UNHOLY

A DARK DOMME ROMANCE

THE DEVIL'S SOCIETY

KINSLEY KINCAID

ISBN eBook: 978-1-998646-01-2

ISBN Paperback: 978-1-998646-06-7

Editing: Rumi Khan

Proofreading: Daisie Mae - Editing & Proofreading

Domme Expert: Gwen Ellis

Cover Design: Artista Grafico

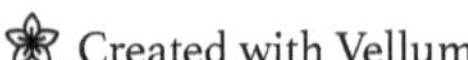 Created with Vellum

NOTE FROM THE AUTHOR

Please be aware this book contains many **dark themes** and subjects that may be uncomfortable/unsuitable for some readers. This book contains **heavy themes** throughout. Please keep this in mind when entering *Unholy*. Content warnings are listed on authors' social pages & website.

This book and its contents are entirely a work of fiction. Any resemblance or similarities to names, characters, organizations, places, events, incidents, or real people are entirely coincidental or used fictitiously.

If you find any genuine errors, please reach out to the author directly to correct it. Thank you.

This book is intended for 18+ only.

READING ORDER

The Devil's Society Series

Elijah's Duet;
Haunted by the Devil
Homecoming
*Sinner; Before Rain - Prequel**

Nathaniel's Story;
Unholy

*Can be read before, between or after the duet.

PLAYLIST

Started - Iggy Azalea
Unholy(feat. Kim Petras) - Sam Smith
Vigilante Shit - Taylor Swift
Crazy In Love - Beyonce
Devil - Niykee Heaton
Church - Chase Atlantic
John Wayne - Lady Gaga
Super Freaky Girl - Nicki Minaj
Pursuit of Happiness - Kid Audi, MGMT, Ratatat, Steve Aoki
Hayloft ll - Mother Mother
Hey Brother - Avicii
Karma - Taylor Swift
Dirty Thoughts - Chloe Adams
House of Memories - Panic! At The Disco
BODY BAG - Neoni

Devil Eyes - Hippie Sabotage

Timber - Pitbull, Kesha

Mastermind - Taylor Swift

Kingslayer - Bring Me The Horizon, BABYMETAL

Bloody Mary - Lady Gaga

Call It What You Want - Taylor Swift

I'll Do It - Sped Up - Heidi Montag

S&M - Rihanna, Britney Spears

Sally(That Girl) - Gucci Crew ll

Playlist

Make them beg for it. You don't owe them shit.

ELIJAH

"D AD!"

"Yes, son. You bellowed?" I hear him shout from his office, sounding sarcastic.

This motherfucker.

It's gone too far this time. I don't need this shit on my phone.

The door to his office is ajar. I throw it open and hear the knob crash into the wall behind it.

"Elijah! Was that really necessary?"

That question is not worthy of a response. My chest heaves as my hand clenches around my phone.

My dad, Nathaniel Sinclair, is standing behind his wooden desk, tattooed hands resting on top with a cigar burning in the ashtray. A crystal glass of whiskey —two fingers, maybe three high—is on a coaster in front of him. He's acting completely oblivious to what I'm here about.

I throw my phone at him, waiting for his gaze to move from me to it.

Twisting my bat in my other hand, I remain standing and wait.

It's a stare-off.

"I could do this all day, old man," I taunt.

The corner of his mouth curls. Challenge accepted.

Our eyes pierce into each other's. The silence adds to the tension.

My phone vibrates against the desk. Lifting my bat into the air, I point it at him, not backing down.

And in that exact moment, I know I have him. Curiosity always killed the cat.

My dad's eyes look down, out of habit, to see who is calling. And in that exact moment, he blinks.

As his focus remains on my phone, his voice is clear and calm, and his words are firm. "Drop it. You don't point that at me in my home. Do you understand?"

I'm pissed off. But he's right. Goddammit.

Giving a subtle nod, I lower my bat and wait for him to inspect the phone.

"It was Rain."

"I'll call her back after you tell me why that shit is on my phone," I say, side-eyeing him.

Lowering to his chair, he adjusts his slacks before

sitting. Wearing a white dress shirt with the sleeves rolled up his forearms and a gold watch adding to the decorations on his inked skin, he reaches for the phone and swipes it open.

A breath of air blows out from between his lips and his head shakes in disbelief. "She really did it."

Leaning back in the chair, a smirk follows, which confuses me since nothing about this is funny.

Taking one more look at the phone, my dad erupts in laughter and chucks the phone back on the wooden desk.

Furious, I threaten to declare war against his best friend. "Tell Delacroix I'll smash the windows of his car if he sends me this shit again."

My statement only sends my dad into a more hysterical fit of laughter.

Taking his gold-framed glasses off, he wipes his eyes from the tears beginning to stream out of them.

"Elijah. This wasn't D. That is his missus."

Jesus fucking Christ. Cheeky bitch, well fucking played.

"Regardless. Whatever shit you all do in your spare time isn't my business. I don't need to see my dad like that," I state while pointing at the phone screen, which shows an image of him and D in silk pajamas, as adults, perhaps even recently, having a pillow fight in some fucking bedroom that I've never seen before.

"She photoshopped it. We haven't done that since

we were kids." My dad is now wheezing with laughter, the same as Rain was when I left our house to come here moments ago.

Throwing my head back, I blow out a sigh of frustration and squeeze my eyes shut. "You do you, Dad. But I don't need to see it. It's fucking weird. I'm your kid!"

"Says the kid who can kill without batting an eye, but a photoshopped picture of his old man is crossing a line?"

Throwing my arms out, I reply, "Abso-fucking-lutely it is."

1

RYLEE

"Fuck, Mistress. Yes."

Moving my black glitter flogger over his bare skin one last time does it, and he comes. His cock pulsates tiny shots of white release onto his stomach.

This client has a tickle fetish.

I keep moving the dangling tassels over his hairy chest while using the long, sharp painted nails of my free hand to circle under his arm as he rides the waves of his short-lived orgasm.

He's always been quick, which I appreciate.

The entire appointment lasts ten minutes. We both leave satisfied, him by coming, and me, I get five hundred dollars to line my pockets.

Stepping back in my knee-high latex heels, I begin to undo the pink metal cuffs locked around his wrists and ankles. My long black hair is slicked back into a high pony; it hangs down to my waist, and I know the ends are tracing his skin, getting him hard while his flesh tingles in satisfaction. But unless he has another five bills, this show is over. But I'm not stupid; this will have him yearning for more, craving me in his dreams, and wishing I was the one getting him off while sitting in a boring fucking board meeting.

It's all about repeat business. Grandma didn't raise a dummy. And if Greta ever heard me call her Grandma, she would throw her bedazzled walker at me.

Yes, I am related to the mysterious and infamous Greta Vandenberg. She's raised me since I was five. My mom, Nic, was fucking stolen from us. I can feel my heartbeat beginning to escalate. Red rage coloring my covered cheeks. I blink rapidly in an effort to clear my mind. Now is not the fucking time.

Walking around the table, the sound of my heels on the hard floor echoes in the silent space. My client still panting, I catch myself in the reflection of the mirrored wall, admiring myself. My body is clad in a black latex bodysuit, arms and bare legs exposed, which my client couldn't give a shit about, but I do. I know I look fucking good. I know I'm a strong bitch and when the time is right, I'll show The Exiled just how bad I can be.

Sweat is still glistening on the man's chest hair, and I remove the restraints.

He isn't in it for the sex, just the pleasure. But he wouldn't be the worst thing I've shoved in my mouth if he were.

"Time's up, you vermin. Now get the fuck off my table and out of my sight," I whisper with disgust dripping off my tongue. He also likes being degraded.

His eyes shoot open. Panic-stricken, he jumps off and gathers his clothing before rushing out the door in just his saggy boxers, which have a wet stain on the front. I chuckle to myself, satisfied with his reaction. He knows if he doesn't listen, I could edge him the entirety of our next session.

"Ry, I have a favor."

Greta's walker can be heard over her gravelly smoker's voice.

Rolling my eyes, I say, "What is it?"

"Ungrateful bitch. Don't roll your eyes at me." Greta knows me better than I know myself. She continues, "Sinclair lost a bet against Delacroix. His dick is nine inches into the glory hole, just fucking hanging there."

"That crazy motherfucker?" I saw what he did to his cousin at Hell Fire Night. How her blood dripped down into the wine goblets as her body hung lifelessly from the aerial ribbons.

"Fuck no. His dad. Rain would cut Elijah's cock off if he even stepped foot in here."

Bending over, I take the cold metal clasps of the

zipper of my boots in both hands and slowly pull them down. I too am a sucker for sensory, the sound of them unzipping; the metal unlatching from each other strangely calms me. Closing my eyes, I take in the few moments of peace it gives me before Greta interrupts.

"I'd do it myself but once I am on my knees, there's not a fucking hope I'd be able to get up. I would even take my dentures out to give him a full experience." Choking on my own spit—that is not the visual I wanted in my head going into this.

"Fuck, Greta. TMI," I mumble under my breath, which causes her to laugh even more. She knows what she's doing, torturing me and loving it.

Sliding my bare feet out of the boots, they fall sideways to the ground. My manicured toes pad over to the open doorway, where Greta is waiting for me.

"Why can't one of the other girls do this?" I question, feeling the cold tiled floor beneath, grounding me.

Blowing out a cloud of cigarette smoke, she replies, "He is a V-I-fucking-P, Rylee. He may hire whores to fuck, but only the best. And you are the only one here he would let near his giant, sacred dick. His other regulars are out on jobs. So you, my lovely granddaughter, are the chosen one today."

I know she's right. Walking ahead of her in the long hallway, I yell back to her, "You are paying me fucking triple for this. And I want a bag, a really expensive bag."

Greta runs the classiest fucking brothel in all of Montana, the entire Midwest, really. This is also our home. Some girls rent a room from us monthly, and others go to the clients' homes and we take a fee for setting up the appointments. But most are independent contractors.

Greta is the head bitch, the house mother, but she hates being referred to as that. I am learning the trade, and one day I will take this over from her, while still being able to do what I love in my playroom.

We cater to the rich, the connected, The Exiled.

Whatever they fantasize, we offer.

And today, Nathaniel Sinclair's fantasy is getting his dick sucked through a hole in the wall.

Turning the black iron doorknob, the door creeks as I take a step in.

Delacroix is sitting in a plush chair, legs wide and stone-faced. He isn't known for his sense of humor. But he is known for being Sinclair's bestie—a very deadly one, in fact.

Smirking at him as I pass, his face doesn't budge to greet me in return. This room has cream shag carpet; my toes curl into the softness of it as I continue to walk toward Sinclair's cock, which is hanging out of the hole. The lights are dimmed, and as I go to kneel down before it, metal shines. My mouth waters—he has piercings. I am surprised his girls have never mentioned this, but I suppose he does make them sign NDAs.

Focusing back to the job, this is something I am not used to, as my knees hit the carpet, because usually they are kneeling before me.

"Have fun," Greta calls into the room as she closes the door.

Clearing my throat, I let curiosity win. "You don't seem like the kind of man who would allow his precious cock to be in this position."

A thump follows; I presume it is his head banging against the wall.

"That motherfucker never wins. This should be his cock in the hole," a deep voice responds back.

A bet.

How interesting. I wonder what he lost.

"I don't do this shit. I never would be here if I didn't have to be." His disclaimer bores me; I couldn't give a fuck as long as I got paid.

"Keep your dick through the hole and shut up." I snap back, and his silence tells me he will obey.

Reaching my hands up to his cock, which is now at eye level, I grip it at the base and squeeze. A faint hiss can be heard from behind the thin wall as he becomes fully erect. My thumb reaches his tip and brushes against one of the cool pieces of metal.

Moving my mouth toward him, I bring my tongue

out and tease him, rubbing it back and forth along his sensitive slit. Precum drips from his head as I bring my lips over it, adding to the agony of need building inside of him. My hands start working him, adding to his desire. The ridges of his additional piercings rub against my palms. He has a ladder, fuck me.

I wonder what it feels like to be fucked by someone with that. It's on my bucket list of things to experience.

My pussy clenches at the thought of all those piercings rubbing against the inside of my cunt.

I decide to stop playing with my meal and slide my lips farther down his thick shaft, taking him as deep as I can. Using my tongue, I continue to tease his underside as I hollow my cheeks and suck him back, hard. My throat does its job, gripping around him tightly as I continue to work him. Saliva builds and begins to drip out of my mouth and down my chin. My lungs are running out of oxygen as I take him out of me and catch my breath.

"Fuck."

Hearing him squirm makes me smile.

My hands move rapidly up and down him, at times pulling on his barbells, which are followed by hisses.

Slowly, I allow a drop of spit to run off my swollen lips and onto his cock, acting as lube for my hands working his shaft. Then, closing my lips, I position his head before them and blow on the tip with my breath.

Which I know is causing his spine to shiver and ass to clench at the sensation.

Wrapping my pouty lips around him once more, I position him so his head rubs against my cheek several times before I take him all the way back. The slam of his hand on the wall startles me, and I know he is on the fucking brink, right where I want him.

My head bobs back and forth rapidly on his cock. I don't gag as I take him deeper. My eyes roll back the farther I get. More drool drips down my chin and onto my chest as my eyes water.

A loud groan erupts from Sinclair as his cock pulsates in my mouth. His warm cum floods my throat, coating it, and I am determined to milk him of every last drop. I don't let up. I squeeze his base harder, and he grunts as more cum shoots out of his cock.

He tastes so fucking good. The salty release is exquisite. This is what elite dick tastes like. Only the fucking best.

I can feel his cock soften as the last drop drips out of him. Pulling back slowly, the once cool metal is now warm in my mouth as my tongue plays with them all before releasing him.

Before letting him out of my grip, I lean forward one last time and kiss his tip, leaving what is left of my black lipstick as a souvenir.

Rising to my feet, his cock remains in the hole, likely as he catches his breath and the stars fade from his vision. Smirking to myself, I know he is seeing stars, who wouldn't be after that?

Turning toward the door, I make my way out, letting the mixture of drool and cum sit on my chin, glistening. Looking up at Delacroix, he is in the same position I left him in. Completely unfazed by what he just witnessed.

Before leaving the room, I turn my head, my long ponytail brushing against my shoulder as I turn to face Delacroix. "What was the bet?" I allow my curiosity to get the best of me.

"None of your fucking business," he snaps back.

I nod in understanding and close the door behind me.

Asshole.

2

NATHANIEL

I swear to fuck if anyone sees me here, I will beat the shit out of Delacroix. Tucking my cock back into my trousers, it's all I can bring myself to think about.

But motherfucker, that was the best blowjob I have ever had. She must be new here, because I can't see Greta holding out on me all this time.

Greta is a mystery to many; some even believe she is an urban legend. A myth.

But not to me. I see her. Really see her.

She is more than the owner of this place that some call a brothel; most call it 'The Ranch'. It's not anything we have discussed before; we have an unspoken respect for one another.

Not many get the luxury of this with her. It's not by coincidence either, Greta is as calculated as I am.

Anytime we make eye contact, a million words are spoken with one look. It's something that just happened one day when Elijah left Montana with his mom all those years ago.

There is a bigger picture at play here, and I am determined to figure it out.

Until then, I will continue to invite her girls into my home every night, then kindly send them away once I am done. Business as usual.

Taking my navy suit jacket off the chair, I slide both arms through and adjust the cuffs of my white dress shirt. I have a rule for myself: always look sharp, never disheveled in public or in front of others. Never show your hand, because if you are having a bad day, they will use it against you.

Unless you are in the inner circle, and I can fucking tell you that my circle is as tiny as my pinkie finger.

Walking to the locked door, I unlatch the chain and open to the hallway, where a gloating Delacroix greets me.

"The man of mystery shows emotion. Is that a smile I see?" Clasping my hands together, I taunt my best friend since childhood. This man got on the dean's list at Harvard, fucking brownnoser; the dean himself called him to congratulate him while D was getting his dick sucked, and all he did was shrug, finish on her face, then hit the showers. I myself was shocked Delacroix knew what a blowjob was, so naturally I stayed to watch and encourage him, which is how I knew this all happened.

So to see him have a tinge of a smile on his face, in this moment, is monumental.

At times, I see a lot of my son, Elijah, in him. It wasn't until that day at the dinner table when Elijah asked, 'What is the best way to kill someone?' did I get it. D and my son are wired differently, but that doesn't mean I can't take the piss out of them.

Rolling his eyes at me, he shoves his hands into his leather jacket pockets and leads us down the dimly lit hallway. It's midday and since most of the activities at The Ranch begin after dark, the house is quiet as we make our way toward the front door. Just as we round the corner, the click of a door behind me catches my attention.

Turning my head, I can see a long black ponytail. It reaches her lower back, which is clad in black shiny latex. Tall knee-high boots are in her tiny hands, and her bare feet pad against the floor. If she feels me looking, she doesn't turn around to check. I stare a bit longer, stopping in my tracks. Absolutely captivated.

Her hips sway with each step as my eyes take her in. As I reach her bare ass, the latex bodysuit being a thong, I can feel my cock react against my trousers. Her long pony sways as I squint harder at her. Why is this so familiar?

My hand scratches at the stubble on my face as a flood of memories rush over me.

It's her.

It fucking has to be.

She came out of the orgy room with such confidence during Hell Fire Night at the cabin, just like she does now.

"Sinclair. Move." D's deep voice grabs hold of my attention.

Blinking my eyes, my focus returns to the present as I pivot on my heels, taking wide steps and reaching the staircase. He doesn't question me once as I catch up; he either didn't notice or doesn't care. Some days his inability to give a shit about certain things drives me absolutely insane, but this time I am thankful.

We both remain quiet as we make it through the rest of the house. A couple girls sit at the bar in the parlor. Glancing over, I give them a curt nod. A couple I recognize from the house calls.

My car is parked out front, and we both get in. Sliding my hand inside of my jacket, I reach for my phone and pull it out. Scrolling through my contacts, I find the one I need.

I want her for the next house call.

GRETA

GRETA REPLIES IMMEDIATELY with a laughing emoji.

Putting my phone away, I put my matte-black Bentley SUV into drive and say, "I hope you took a picture, this is the one time you and your missus are ever winning a bet."

He doesn't respond, instead pulling out his own phone, likely messaging Cecilia.

It turns out Elijah did in fact destroy D's Range.

I called him after my son left, telling him what his missus accomplished, then D baited me with, 'Want to bet?' This one time, he knew my son better than I did.

The next morning, I got a bunch of pictures of the Range Rover's tinted windows gone emailed to me. Even the front windshield was destroyed. Dents decorated the outside. That is when I knew I was fucked. He never wins, and they were not going to go easy on me with this time.

Well fucking played.

The drive home is quiet. As much as this experience has been less than ideal, it has taken my mind off one thing.

The Exiled.

So much shit has changed since Hell Fire. My son and his girlfriend, Rain, have been initiated; she found out they are expecting, and now shit is getting messy within the society. Not because of them. It's been since that night, though, and I can feel it. Tides are changing, rumors are swirling, and unease riddles my bones.

I continue driving through town, and before I know it, I am pulling up to Delacroix's. Parking, he starts to get out, but before closing the door, he bends down and flashes his phone at me. Leaning over, I see a picture of my dick in the glory hole on the screen, before the girl came in.

A loud chuckle erupts from my mouth. "Well fucking done, brother," I praise.

D responds back, "I know." Then he shuts the door.

Before taking off for home, another text comes through, the vibration against my chest alerting me to it.

UNKNOWN:

New World Order.

3

RYLEE

I'm back in my bedroom, which is located in the private wing of the house. The Ranch is my childhood home. Growing up, from what I can tell in pictures, my mom tried to make it as normal and cut off from the business side as possible. Then, after she passed, Greta did, and she managed to keep it that way. Many of the girls here are family to me. If Greta was busy they helped take care of me. This life is all I know. These incredibly strong and powerful women helped mold me into the woman I am today. I wouldn't change my upbringing for anything.

Greta also has her living quarters here. It's the one place we are able to escape, if only for a few moments. We have a kitchen area, but we aren't one to have family dinners.

Out back, the old swing set and sandbox I played in

remain. Some girls will bring their kids here during the day, let them play while they set up their rooms for the evening clients or collect paychecks.

The house is large and has been in our family since my grandmother's parents bought it when she was a child. Back then, it was just a home. Once they passed, Greta inherited it and turned this place into something exquisite. It's where we can all come together and be ourselves for an evening. A place where we are safe to do what we love.

It's 2025; slut-shaming will get you banned before you even step foot into The Ranch, and we aren't opposed to a little harm, should the crime fit.

We live in a town where rules and laws are merely suggestions. I suppose The Exiled did one thing right. They control the police, the judges, and district attorneys. Brothels aren't technically legal in Montana, so the last thing anyone is going to do is call the police in the event of suspected foul play.

At The Ranch, experimenting is encouraged and giving in to temptation and desires is a must. This is where I was free to give in to my dormant side. Greta has always said since I was a little girl, *'Embrace who you are; don't hide from it or run. Chase your dreams, because if you don't, it will only catch up to you in the form of regret. You have one life; regret shouldn't be a thought. Living freely should be.'*

Throwing my boots to the ground, I walk into my en suite and go immediately for the mouthwash.

I hate The Exiled. I fucking despise them.

I want to vomit.

Greta knows my stance on them, but still, she asked me to do the unthinkable to that monster. Perhaps she thought it was best to keep them happy than to be on their radar.

My face cringes at the memory of sucking his cock while being watched by his equally vile friend; it makes my stomach turn. That fucker, Darian, whose loyalty to his precious society has always baffled me. He forced his now wife, Cecilia, to marry him on Hell Fire Night. They threaten death if you don't obey.

Her father would be turning in his grave.

Why? Because The Exiled killed him, the same way they eliminated Darian's family.

Indirectly, they also caused her mother's death—a car accident. And yet she still chose life over death. Turning her back on her principles for the sake of being able to see the next day.

Coward.

Rinsing my mouth out with the minty fresh wash, I spit the blue liquid into the sink and watch it trickle down the drain.

Looking up, I see myself in the mirror. My makeup is a mess. Black mascara running down my cheeks and lipstick worn off and smudged, stained around my mouth.

Moving my tongue gently along the inside of my cheek, I swear I can still feel his head pushing against it with the silver barbells leaving an imprint.

My sharp canines bite the inside of my lip, and my eyes hood as my mouth fills with saliva. The memory of his musky scent follows. My pussy tingles under my tight latex bodysuit, pulsating and begging me to grind against something. Desire moves up my body. I can feel my nipples harden; they are desperate to be pinched and pulled. The pads of my fingers barely touch my body, but electricity follows, dancing seductively with every inch I move. Reaching my throbbing cunt, I cup it tightly, and my pelvis takes control, slowly moving and rubbing my clit against the cool latex.

The nerves ignite as I chase what I crave. My head gets heavy, and my neck allows it to follow backward. With hooded eyes, I picture him, his cock, and how fucking phenomenal it feels rubbing against my tight walls. They tighten, trying to grip the cock my mind is seeing. A soft moan brushes against my lips, triggering my hips to move faster; the wetter I get, the more the latex squeaks against my hand.

I can feel my body getting warmer, causing my bodysuit to stick to my skin. It feels tighter the more I pant.

No.

Disgust returns to my mouth, and my stomach drops.

Immediately I freeze, stopping the chase.

Throwing my head back up, I look in the mirror and take myself in. "He is the goddamn enemy," I whisper to myself, absolutely mortified.

Gripping the countertop, my body folds and my head falls on the cool marble in shame. Closing my eyes, I take a couple deep breaths in. My heart is beating in my ears in disbelief that I had a moment of weakness.

I nearly got off on him. What is wrong with me?

As much as I want to ride his ladder, it's not worth going against everything I believe in.

A knock on my door startles me. I nearly jump out of my skin. Balling my hands into fists, my long black fingernails poke into the palms of my hands. I don't move.

Another loud knock follows.

Picking myself up, I try to fix the baby hairs and frizz that have since developed due to my lack of self-respect and control.

Next, the knob begins to rattle. The door is locked; they won't get in.

Blowing out a deep sigh, I pad across the room and toward the door. The cool brass against my warm skin is refreshing as I turn the knob slowly. Opening the large white door, I peek through the slender crack and take in the one person I wish wasn't standing on the other side right now.

Greta.

"We need to talk," she abruptly snarks out at me.

Four words that never lead to anything good.

Blowing out a deep sigh, I open the door farther, inviting her inside. My toes curl in the plush black carpet as Greta makes her way past me. Once in, I swing the door closed behind her and hop to my king-size bed. White blankets with large white fluffy pillows decorate it, and a soft black cashmere throw is draped overtop.

Before tucking myself underneath the throw, I remove my tight and sticky latex and toss it toward my closet. Greta has seen worse; getting naked in front of her isn't anything to be embarrassed about. As I get comfortable, I wait for her to take a seat on my black velvet oversized chair. It's where she always sits when visiting me.

I watch as she gets comfortable, and I catch her glancing at me. Her face gives nothing away, always miserable. I haven't a clue why she's here.

Skipping formalities, Greta gets straight to the point once she has cleared her throat. "You're going to see him tomorrow night. House call."

Excuse me?

Instantly, my body reacts. Sitting up, my eyes widen

in disbelief. "Not a fucking chance." Greta rolls her eyes at my response, unfazed by my objection.

"No. No, you don't get to say that, then roll your eyes at me. I go along with some crazy shit. Anything you ask, I do it, always without a fight. But not this. Never fucking this." My chest is heaving with anger, and my hands softly tremble.

How could she? Emotion wells in my eyes.

If anyone should hold content against The Exiled, it's her, then me as a close second. Fuck her for even thinking I would consider this.

"Ry, he has requested you. You've made an impression," she follows up casually while reaching into her pocket for her pack of cigs.

Shaking my head, I reply, "I don't do house calls. I don't do vanilla. You know that. Does he? Or did you forget to inform him when agreeing I would do this?" I probe, raising my brow at her.

Flipping her lighter open, the flame ignites as she lights the cigarette, a long, skinny one hundred. Then taking a deep inhale, Greta looks me dead in the eye as she blows the smoke out, slowly with intent of showing me she isn't fucking around.

She keeps the flame going.

Shaking her head at me, this level of intimidation is not something I have witnessed from her before. "You think he has never heard of you? Stupid girl."

Greta pauses; her tone changed, something I rarely see firsthand.

At times, she has to be firm with the girls if they have fucked up, or she is a straight-up asshole back to the men who think they own the place, but this is aerie. After taking another inhale, she continues. "Bigger things are at play here. Things that you could barely start to comprehend. Keep him close. If you ever want to take this business over, you must listen to me. Hear everything I am not saying. Do you fucking understand me?"

Her last statement stings. And my trembling hands stop. Silence engulfs the space as I absorb it all. My eyes shift back and forth around my room, not focusing on anything but seeing everything as my brain becomes frantic trying to decipher her cryptic words.

What is she talking about? Hell Fire Night just happened; what more could be happening?

As a million different scenarios flood my mind, I don't even notice Greta and her glitter walker walking to the door. It isn't until I hear the floor creak under her step that it catches my attention.

My head jolts, turning to face her. Greta is now standing in the doorway. She doesn't move, continuing to look out into the hallway.

Just as I think she is about to leave, she speaks. Her words come out hard and firm, but worry and fear are also noticeable. "There are things you aren't privy to. But it appears the day is coming where you will be. I need you to be on alert when leaving the safety of this property. Be aware of your surroundings and call me if you sense anything off."

As her last word is spoken, she continues into the hall and disappears. My body feels heavy because of the unknown. Energy changes have always physically impacted me. Pressure against my chest gets stronger the longer her words linger in my thoughts.

Picking my nail polish is a habit I have when my anxiety comes knocking. Instead of getting lost in it, I focus on my breathing, the sound of my heart, and the feeling of my soft blanket between my fingers. By the time I bring myself back and calm down, most of my fingernails have been affected. But then it clicks.

This could work to my advantage.

Greta is onto something.

Tapping my chin with my finger I get an idea.

It may not be her intent, but I can't help the pull I feel to this thought.

The Exiled killed my mother. And now I will kill them from the inside out.

I smirk to myself.

Nathaniel Sinclair, how may I be of service?

4

RYLEE

The road is dark; the only lights besides my headlights come from the bright moon above. Music is playing through my speakers as I rev my engine harder. The loud roar is followed by a smooth purr. I fucking love this car.

It's an Aston Martin One-77. Only seventy-seven were made, and I have one. This town is full of money and greed; people have offered me millions for it, but I will never part with her. I used some of my inheritance from my mom to get it. My mom is—was—worth more than this car and all the money in the world could ever mean to me, but having this is like having a tiny piece of her with me. It's invaluable, so no amount of money or persuasion could ever make me part with her.

I remember when I first saw the Aston, it was on some television show I was watching with her before she passed. I was five. It wasn't this model, but she said, *'Now that's a car.'* It stayed with me for years as a comfort memory. One would pass in the streets or be parked in the lot at the grocery store, and I would hear her voice whispering to me, *Now that's a car.*

One day I heard they were making the One-77, a rarity I had to have because Mom was a rarity to me, like a pink diamond.

It wasn't until my inheritance kicked in that I could even imagine affording one, but to have one would allow me to keep her memory close to me. I know it's materialistic, but grief and healing are different for all, and this is my way to deal with them.

I would periodically scroll the internet for any sign of one on sale, to the point I almost lost hope. Then, an estate sale overseas had their catalog online for browsing. There she was, my pink diamond. I bid relentlessly until I got it. I nearly cried from the stress, but the relief of winning took over. It was immediately shipped over to Bozeman, and I am never letting her go. That all happened after the last Hell Fire, five years ago.

I'm not sure why that is significant, but five years later something is shifting; I feel it in my gut. The odds of all the events leading up to now, driving to Nathaniel Sinclair's, aren't a fluke. And like my pink diamond, I will be on the right side of history, again.

Turning onto Sinclair's secluded and private road, an iron gate awaits me. Standing out front are multiple security men, which isn't unusual for a man of his stature, but with his psychotic son back, I'm surprised he needs this many still. Coming to a stop, the engine still purrs as I roll down my window. One man walks up, wearing all black paired with a black mask covering the bottom part of his face. Knowing me, my face is loudly expressing how absurd I think it is.

"Name," he says abruptly, with zero people skills.

Batting my lashes, I play the part as many others from The Ranch have in the days and years past. "Rylee Vandenberg, Greta sent me," I tell him, smiling.

Bringing his wrist to his mouth, the man in black radios someone above his pay grade, repeating my name. Another man takes a scanner and walks around my car, holding it close, as a third man does the same but to the underneath. If I wanted to sneak anything in with my car, that is out of the question now.

Moments pass, and I begin to get bored and frankly debate closing my eyes for a quick nap. Before I can act on it, the large gate slowly starts to open, and my new friend gives me a nod, allowing me to enter the estate. Rolling my window up, I take a deep breath and proceed forward. A couple streetlights line the area, and large trees allow for privacy, restricting my ability to properly take in the area. And all Greta told me about this evening was that Nathaniel's house is on the left.

Looking to my right, chills tingle down my spine,

and goosebumps cover my bare arms as Elijah's house comes into view. I am not scared or intimidated by him, but his unpredictability and lack of remorse does put me slightly on edge.

My eyes trail up and down his property. Black-domed cameras surround the place. If his place is that secure, fuck knows Nathaniel's must be too. Glancing to my left, lights illuminate the driveway that I slowly turn onto. The two-story home is incredible; the exterior is a mix of wood and stone and two front entrances with a large garage off to the side and fencing to the other, and more trees and shrubbery decorate the area. Looking up at one of the posts, immediately I notice more cameras.

If they have this many cameras, they must have sensors too. Security here is like nothing I have seen before, with the exception of the King, who is the leader of The Exiled.

No one is getting into the estate unless invited. It's a fortress.

Pulling up to the first door, I stop, parking my car.

This is it.

Swiping my small handbag from the passenger seat, I open the car door. Swinging my black stiletto-clad feet out, I stand, pulling down my black strapless bandage dress, which barely covers my ass, and close the door behind me. Looking up, I am startled by an older gentleman who is now standing before me in a black suit and black clipboard in hand.

"Before you enter, you will need to read and sign this document. Once signed, it also grants me permission to search your handbag and complete a handheld metal detector scan of your body," he explains, holding the clipboard out.

The driveway is lit with plenty of light. As I take the board, my eyes skim the document, and it's then I realize it's an NDA. We make clients sign them at The Ranch, so it's only right he has one for his home. Standard fucking procedure in the corrupt town of Bozeman.

I flip to the last page and hold my free hand out without looking up. A black pen is placed into it, and I sign my life away. Giving his clipboard and pen back, he grabs the detector from under his arm. "Legs apart and arms up."

"Charming. Does all this foreplay usually get the others wet?" Sarcasm drips from my words.

His face doesn't budge as he scans my body for weapons of mass destruction. Once completed, he nods to my bag, which I open so he can rummage through it. His fingers wrap around my phone, taking it out. "Mine until you leave."

Blowing out a sigh of frustration, I don't argue.

"You may enter. Master Sinclair will be waiting for

you in his study," are his last words to me as he turns on his heel and walks away.

But that doesn't stop me from shouting, "Because I know where that is."

Walking up to the large wooden door, my hand grips the iron handle and pushes it open. Taking a step inside, I am welcomed with the smell of warm vanilla. Closing my eyes, I take a deep breath in. It's my favorite scent.

A deep voice interrupts my moment of peace. "Down here."

Nathaniel.

Opening my eyes, I bring myself inside, closing the door gently behind me.

And with the click of the latch, it occurs to me that if I am going to kill him, getting anything in here to do so will be nearly impossible.

Well played, Sinclair, but I can play better and smarter.

Smirking to myself, I make my way down to him. The front entrance is large; you can see the back of the house from here. Large windows allow the moonlight through; the silhouette of the mountainscape can faintly be seen beyond the lush tree line. Stairs are on the right to me, and as I peer up, a balcony going left shows itself. Dim lights line the walls, adding to the ambience already set by the vanilla scent. My heels click against the flooring, echoing, making my arrival to his office door known.

His deep voice greets me. "Come in."

Stepping through the threshold, I catch myself, biting the inside of my lip, but I stop myself before he sees and takes it for a weakness, even if it's not. Men like him will take the smallest thing and manipulate it against you.

Confidently with my shoulders back and chest out, I add a hint of swing to my hips while my eyes move up, taking in the very masculine space. Dark leathers and wood fill the room; a bar is off to the side with a bookshelf lining the wall behind my host. A large, dark desk sits before me as I continue moving toward him. My eyes find his crystal glass of whisky, which has a lit cigar sitting in the ashtray next to it.

Tattooed hands meet the glass, his fingers wrap around it, and my eyes follow it up as he moves it to his lips. Watching, he takes a sip, his Adam's apple moving as he swallows. His jawline is shaded with a mixture of salt-and-pepper facial hair that is perfectly manicured. Wandering upward, my eyes find his, and I curse internally. Why do men always have the best lashes?

Deep lines surround his eyes, showing endless days and nights of stress. And then his dark brown orbs, which are hidden behind a thick pair of black glasses, penetrate mine in return. I don't allow mine to linger there long; they move up to his full head of thick, graying hair. It's untamed, as if he has just thrown his fingers through it moments before I entered.

What's on your mind, old man?

"Like what you see?" His words come out slow and seductive. Smooth like the aged whisky he is indulging in.

"Hardly. Rude to not offer your guest a refreshment," I throw back.

Placing his glass on the desk, Nathaniel rises, and my breath hitches. My eyes move back down his face and thick neck to his strong, defined shoulders. This motherfucker knows my weakness as I take him in further. Ink decorates his chest and abdomen that reveals a six-pack underneath. Then, I see the Adonis lines leading to his cock that has the seven pieces of silver through it. But it is currently covered by a pair of gray sweatpants that are hugging him in all the right places.

Faintly I hear a chuckle, but don't let it bother me. "Just seeing what I have to work with," I coyly retort. But it doesn't stop there. Walking around his desk, his feet are bare and equally as covered in black inked designs. I give my head a slight shake to bring my mind back into focus, and as I do, Nathaniel has made it to his bar, where his strong arms flex while picking up the whisky bottle. He pours me two fingers, then walks over in front of me, holding it out. My fingers grip the crystal at the bottom so as not to touch his. Bringing it to my red lips, I take a swig of my own.

The flavors are tantalizing, full-bodied, and rich. Pairs incredibly well with the vanilla scent he has filled the home with. A hint of clove and honey can be tasted once swallowed, leaving a warm feeling in my mouth. Looking up at my host, I ask, "Thirty years?"

The corner of his mouth smirks. "Precisely, Ms. Vandenberg."

Deeply inhaling through my nose, there is an added layer, his musky sandalwood aroma invading my senses.

He knows exactly what he is doing. A bachelor. Sure, he was married once, but that ended in divorce, and I hear he wasn't faithful anyhow.

"I saw you that night, at Hell Fire, coming out of the orgy room. Wearing nothing but your shiny latex mask, hair slicked back in a pony like now, and pasties covering your hard nipples." Nathaniel takes another step toward me, the tip of his toes brushing against mine. "Was your pussy as wet then as it is now?"

A tiny giggle passes my lips. "You must be mistaken, Mr. Sinclair. My pussy is dry as a bone."

Reaching his hand up, he takes the glass out of mine. "If I were to check, it would tell me you are lying," he taunts before taking the last swig of my whisky for himself.

He isn't wrong, but I won't allow him to call me out on my bluff.

"What am I doing here, Mr. Sinclair? Surely, you have heard my tastes are well above the standard cravings," I question, genuinely curious about his answer.

Stepping back, he breaks the invisible hold this moment has on both of us. His backside leans against his desk, and the empty glass is placed next to him. He crosses his feet at the ankles and grips the edge firmly. "Your mouth around my cock. And this time leave some of that pretty red on him," he responds with a wink.

Looking around, I realize I could break a multitude of bottles and stab him relentlessly mid-blowjob, ending his life embarrassingly. So many precautions to enter, but very little in place once I have entered.

Tossing my bag onto the brown leather couch, I step forward, my body pressing against his. My teeth tug on his lobe before whispering, "As you wish, Mr. Sinclair."

He remains still, acting unaffected, but I can feel his heart racing against my chest.

Taking my sharp nails, I bring them to his chest, where a thin patch of white hair allows for them to get tangled. They scratch both his erect nipples as they move down. Gently, I keep scraping them against his skin and the ridges of his abs as I reach the path to his cock that is nicely defined by his muscles. My fingers linger along his waistline, toying and teasing him.

I feel his cock rising, getting harder the more I play. My mouth waters at the thought of having him in my mouth again.

Slowly lowering myself, my eyes look up, watching him as he watches me.

Wasting no time, my fingers wrap under his waistband and pull the sweatpants down to his ankles. Nathaniel's cock springs out, light catches it, and the silver jewelry glints in the dim room. My hands grip him tightly, appearing small in comparison, so I use both to fully wrap around his thick shaft. I let a string of spit slide from my mouth, down my lips and chin, then onto his head. He hisses from the sensitivity of it.

"Make it filthy, Ms. Vandenberg," he instructs, even though I had every intention of doing so.

Working his hard cock with my hands, I move up and down his smooth shaft. The ridges of his piercings give me an idea. I tug on a few, gripping my hands tighter as I move over them. Looking up, Nathaniel's eyes are hooded as he watches, and a deep growl comes from his throat.

Placing my lips over his shaft, my tongue teases his slit, and precum is already leaking from him.

Measured and deliberately, I allow my teeth to scrape down his length. As I bring them back forward to his tip, my canines get caught on the barbells and tug him harder than my hands did.

One hand rapidly comes forward and takes a hold of my pony, right at the base. It's a warning, but I have always played on the dangerous side.

Saliva builds inside my mouth. I am not swallowing it, instead letting it drip all over his cock and down my chin and onto my breasts. Then, in one swift movement, he pushes my head forward, forcing his cock down my throat. Unprepared, I gag as more drool streams from me.

"Choke on me," he demands, still ramming himself farther down.

The gagging doesn't stop; my eyes are watering, and my lips have reached his pelvis.

"You really are filthy, aren't you, Ms. Vandenberg?" he praises.

He has no fucking idea.

The mixture of his precum and saliva dance along my tongue. I hate how good he tastes and feels. The cool metal is now warm against the inside of my mouth and throat. Taking the tip of my tongue, I tickle the underside of his shaft before he finally releases my hair. Placing my hands on the ground next to me, I allow my mouth to continue doing all the work.

My eyes notice his stomach contracting, and it makes my pussy tingle in gratification. My focus stays on him, while Nathaniel's eyes barely remain open as we keep eye contact.

Relaxing my throat, I pull back, gradually allowing his cock to release back into my mouth. With puckered lips, I hollow my cheeks and suck his head, hard. Another hiss leaves him. I glance at his hands and they are squeezing the wooden edge of the desk so tightly that his veins are showing. Another wave of satisfaction washes over me and goes right to my clit, aching to be played with while I play with him. The taste of his cock is as rich as the whisky that graced my palate only moments ago. Combined, the two flavors have turned me into a fiend.

Gradually moving up his shaft once more, his head passes down the back of my throat, and I suck him harder, making my throat contract. At the same time, I can feel my pussy leaking, and there is nothing I can do to stop it.

Tears trickle down my cheeks from the lack of oxygen, and my lungs are desperate, but I don't care; I will not stop until he coats me in his release.

Nathaniel's voice is husky as he taunts me, "I fucking knew it. You like my cock in your mouth. Desperate for it, my precious puppet. Suck it, baby."

Puppet has me furious, then the *baby* speaks to my pussy and I can't help it. Raising my hands, I work his shaft vigorously. His abs contract further; he is nearly there.

My legs begin to tremble, hopefully unnoticed.

"Take it all. No spitting," he demands as his warm cum coats my throat. He tastes so fucking good, the salty release mixed with the metallic taste of the metal and his soft skin.

I'm becoming an addict.

My pussy is begging to grind on anything. I squeeze my pelvic floor, kegeling, in an effort to give it what it needs.

Saliva still overwhelms my mouth even though I am swallowing every last drop he is giving me, yet some still is dripping down my body and onto my chest.

"Your tits are fucking covered, Puppet. I want to slide my cock through them next."

Cum is still shooting out as I move his head to my mouth, my lips wrapped tightly around him as my tongue plays. My ovaries are tingling as my pussy pulsates.

On trembling legs, my own release washes over me, but I don't stop pleasuring him. I squeeze my thighs together, putting more pressure on my swollen pussy lips. It feels so fucking good.

The last bit of release from him coats my mouth as I remove him completely. A string of cum is still connected from his head to my lips, and I don't want to break it.

His hand comes to my face as I watch his softening cock bob.

Nathaniel's thumb circles the one side of my cheek, smudging the tears and streaks of mascara.

"Such a good fucking girl, Puppet," he praises. "I see you liked that too," he adds with a wink.

My top teeth bite my lip, the cum string breaks, and my senses start coming back to me. I am absolutely pissed for allowing myself to get caught up in him, again.

I saw him that night at Hell Fire, but I will never confirm that to him. I need him to feel like he was just another man, nothing worth remembering.

I am lost in my rush of thoughts when the silence is broken by the sound of his phone vibrating endlessly on his desk.

He doesn't move to reach for it, keeping his gaze on me. I don't react either, instead allowing the words laced with venom to murmur from between my swollen lips. "I hate you," I seethe. He needs to know none of this is from lust. I used him as much as he used me.

And I am no one's fucking puppet.

Rising to my feet, I brush the underside of my bottom lip with my thumb, removing any remaining cum or saliva before turning to leave.

He catches me off guard, his tone casual and arrogant. "You hate the institution, and me by default. Don't confuse the two. And it's Duke to you, Ms. Vandenberg. I'll be seeing you again."

5

NATHANIEL

I see right through her, but I will allow her to continue to think otherwise.

She loved giving me that blowjob as much as I enjoyed getting it. And no fucking chance she hates me; the wet puddle left behind by her pussy would beg to differ.

Chuckling to myself, I lean back in my chair, sucking back on my cigar, and check my phone to see who felt the need to annoy me this evening. Before I am able to, Rogers pokes his head in. "Sir, I have the information you requested."

"Email me everything," I instruct. He responds with a curt nod and walks away.

Rogers is family; he has been the estate manager since I bought the place. I trust him with everything. He has never betrayed me or the family.

Picking my phone up, it goes off displaying his email. I ignore it for now, instead finding the mystery caller and dialling them back. It rings four times before a younger man's voice answers. "Duke, we need a cleanup crew. Dalton, he just fucking lost it. So many bodies, blood everywhere. The chief of police among them. Duke, what do we do?"

Keeping my tone calm, I say, "Where?"

"Hell Fire cabin," the kid stutters in response.

Confused, I reply, "What are people doing at the cabin?"

The line goes quiet; heavy breathing only remains, so I ask another question. "Is he still there?"

"Yes."

Shit.

"I'm on my way," is all I say being hanging up.

On Hell Fire Night, we were told the King was dead —Dalton's father, Brad. Then conflicting information followed through stating otherwise. None of us have seen Brad, so to say I was suspicious would be a fucking understatement at this point. The fucker has been peacocking around town for weeks; this is the first town official he has taken out. What in the hell is he thinking?

Slamming my hands down on my desk, now is the only time I allow my frustrations to show. In the privacy of my home, in my office.

Next, I message Delacroix.

. . .

ME

Need you at the Hell Fire cabin. Call
the crew. I'll call E.

D

Understood.

I DIAL ELIJAH NEXT; he picks up after the first ring. "What?"

"Son, I've missed you too. How's Rain and the baby?" He hates small talk; it only drives my need to do it more knowing that.

"Fine. What do you want?"

"Can't a father call to check in on his son? I am so proud of you. I don't tell you enough." He is gearing to punch me through the phone; I can feel it with the lack of response. Faintly, I can hear Rain laughing in the background. I really like her, love her even, for Elijah. She helps balance him, if that's possible.

"Apologize to Rain for me, I need you at the cabin… Dalton," I explain. And saying *his* name is all I need to do. My son isn't one for formalities; the call ends, and moments later I hear him revving his engine from across the street and squealing his tires as he takes off.

Elijah has been keeping an eye on him casually since his cock-up at The Ranch. He tried to rough up one of the girls when they became uncomfortable, then he wouldn't leave after the session was completed. Dalton pinned her against the wall, but she was able to reach one of many panic buttons calling for help. Security rushed in and threw him out immediately.

That little shit thinks too highly of himself.

And the police is my fucking territory, along with judges and hits.

After the incident at Greta's, I asked if the Antichrist could do some digging, low-key. The King's son has always been an arrogant prick, but since Hell Fire he has amped up all efforts, which makes me believe that his father is truly dead.

Not many are aware Greta runs the rebel group; I don't think her granddaughter is even privy to such information. For her to complete surveillance on him is a lot easier than it is for Elijah and I. We can observe, but she can get deeper. If we get close, red flags would go up immediately and would impact any efforts from the Antichrist.

Standing up, I turn around and pull on one of the bookcases. It swings open like a door, revealing a wall of weapons and a change of clothes. Quickly I switch out my sweats for black trousers and throw on a white button-up dress shirt and black jacket. Reaching for my Glock, I slide that into the back of my pants and close the case.

Then, grabbing my phone, I send Greta a text before heading out.

Again. Tomorrow.

~

PULLING UP TO THE CABIN, my brother from another mother is waiting outside, looking thrilled. He and my son are so fucking similar. Yet they couldn't be more different. It truly is an interesting dynamic to observe.

Parking the Range Rover, I jump out and meet Delicroux around the other side.

"Your kid is ready to slaughter. His pacing is making the cleaners uneasy," he explains as we walk into the cabin.

"Is *he* still here?" I question, taking in the sight before me. It's fucking carnage. What in the hell went on here?

"Negative. The commoner who called you said *he* left shortly after his call to you."

Walking through the entrance and past where goblets of blood would be resting on Hell Fire, we follow the sound of the commotion.

Elijah is pacing, twisting his bat with his wrist, and only stopping when he spots me enter.

He points to the wall and shouts, "The asshat is taunting us."

My eyes go to what he's focused on.

Fuck.

KING is written in capital letters using blood on the white wall.

Is he confirming our beliefs? Does he know we have other eyes on him? Are we being bugged?

All questions that I need Rogers on because this isn't a coincidence.

My face is neutral as thoughts race frantically through my mind. Casually I shift my eyes, examining the room and the other members in attendance; anything and everyone here is significant.

Ignoring my son, I command the room, "Anyone left alive?" not wanting to draw further attention our way.

"Just the one who called you," an eager member speaks up, wanting to show his worth using his knowledge.

Turning my head to the bloody scene before us, I ask, "What are *they* still doing here?" while walking over to the now deceased chief of police. Kneeling, I take in the body, a single close-range gunshot to the back of the head, dead instantly.

Executed.

"We didn't want to move them until you got here, Duke," the member continues. My eyes continue to surveillance the area, noting that the blood has already begun to dry on the floor. "What's your name, kid?"

You can hear his chest push out with confidence. "Thomas."

He's one of Greta's. I knew he looked familiar. She has Antichrist members all over. Faces who blend in, never raising suspicion, are easier to insert, like Thomas. He's never been to Hell Fire, nor to a meeting, but no one in this room is challenging whether he belongs.

She isn't doing this to spy on us, but to gather intel on the increased events and fucking chaos since Hell Fire Night.

Giving him a curt nod, I command the room as I rise, "Clear the room!" Everyone scurries except for Elijah and Delicroux.

Once everyone is gone, my hands rest in my trouser pockets. Walking up to my best friend, I whisper in his ear, "D, call Ryder. Tell them we are going to leave the body in plain sight. We have an internal situation but can't have the town suspicious. They need to believe this is between us and them. Corrupt chief. Uneasiness brings unpredictability. We need to portray that we have this contained. They'll understand. This kid is taunting us, there is no longer a doubt in my mind that Brad, our former King, is dead."

If the other members of The Exiled have

suspected, none have been vocal about it. Fear is most likely fueling their silence.

Turning to my son, my tone is firm when I say, "Not. Yet." His chest heaves, hungry for bloodshed. His tongue moves across his teeth and newly implanted sharp canines, which Rain got him as a gift that he made permanent.

Elijah craves blood and inflicting pain. Withdrawal hits hard when he can't get it. *But soon, son, soon, I fucking promise.*

Stomping out of the room, he purposefully steps in the pool of blood that's not yet dry as he goes to leave.

"He'll survive," I mumble to myself. I hate having a leash on him. I never want to hold him back, but we have to be smart.

Clapping my hands together, I call out to the banished team. "Clean this shit up. Leave the chief's body in Ryder's territory. The others, unmarked graves. Understood?"

As they hustle back into the space, "Yes, Duke" is said quietly as they scurry to get to work.

Thomas is standing just in my peripheral view. "Supervise the cleanup, kid." I trust my cleanup team, but I need to make sure I truly can. Thomas will tell me if my gut is right.

Before turning to leave, I see D casually pass Thomas and whisper something I can't hear, but see the kid say, "Understood."

Leading the way, I take in the bloodied *KING* scrawled on the wall one last time. He knew I could barely tolerate his father, and him, nothing more than a fucking immature peacocking child, not equipped to run a fucking billion-dollar organization.

If he wants to play, I'll fucking play. And I'll win because I'm better at this game than he is.

6

RYLEE

Thin leather straps crack against my skin. Blunt ends penetrating, stinging, and marking my body. I jolt forward, cowardly, on the edge of my bed with each whip.

I pride myself on discipline. But tonight I broke my own cardinal rule: giving in to my own pleasure. I lost control, I failed myself, and I must pay the consequences.

Five lashings are all I allow myself before stopping.

Laying the whip on the bed before me, I move my fingers between the tangled straps, lining them perfectly next to one another before starting again.

Instinct wants me to hiss, but I resist.

It would only add more lashings to my current count.

No one makes me do this but myself. My standards

for myself are high, and I've failed. I deserve this. It's the only way I can become the best version of myself.

The blunt ends of the industrial staples hit an already existing wound. My eyes prickle with pain. Crying isn't acceptable, nor is it an option.

Five more lashings complete, then I repeat the process with intent to do five more when a knock at the door stops me.

Resting my forehead on my bed, I take a couple deep breaths and gather my composure before allowing life outside of this room to exist, again.

With hands clasped around the warm leather handle, I slide it under my blankets as I rise. My hair is still up. Having removed my makeup prior, I can feel my warm cheeks, which means there may be injuries. Grabbing my sleep tee, I slide it over my naked body, the hem reaching just under my bottom, and pad toward the door. Another knock breaks the silence. This time it's harder and louder. Blowing out one last deep breath, I grip the metal knob and slowly open the door.

Greta looks up at me. A cig is hanging out of her mouth as her hands grip her walker.

"Tomorrow. He wants to see you again. You're making an impression," her gravelly voice informs me.

Shaking my head, I say, "Absolutely not." I'm adamant.

"Too fucking bad." Her phone rings before she's

able to continue her guilt trip. She answers quickly, "What happened?"

My brows rise with curiosity.

"No, stay there. Do as they say. I'm putting another guy on the house." Her tone is authoritative, but for the life of me, I can't figure out what she's talking about or to whom. There is a long silence before she continues. "Thomas, observe everything. It's all important, and stick close to them; you can learn a lot from those two," is the last thing she says before hanging up.

Greta puts her phone away and then in quick succession, puts out her cig on the doorframe just to light another. "Jesus fucking Christ," I hear her natter under her breath.

I lean against the doorframe, observing her. It's like she has forgotten I'm even here as her eyes focus on the floor, like she's thinking and strategizing. Lost in a daze of thoughts.

It's what she does; I've seen this face a million times. Never understanding what could be raising through her mind.

Greta's head nods, and her eyes begin to blink again. "You are going. And be fucking careful. Message me once you arrive, then leave," she demands.

Bewildered by it all, I simply nod my head and whisper, "Yeah, okay."

Satisfied, Greta turns around and continues down

the hall, not another word spoken before she disappears.

Closing my door, I hear the latch click and turn my back to it. Sliding down the hardwood, my knees bend as my backside meets the plush carpet.

My back stings as I apply pressure on it while at the same time feeling so fucking good. My eyes shift around the room as I try to piece together all the tiny clues Greta has given me. But the tiny breadcrumb trail is still too vague.

Hell Fire Night has passed. The bikers have kept to themselves. The Exiled are The Exiled. They own this fucking town; no one dares to challenge that unless they want to die.

There haven't been any alerts on my phone about anything happening in town. Tilting my head up with mixed emotions, I haven't a fucking clue, other than I know I have to see Sinclair again.

PULLING INTO THE SECURE STREET, I pass Elijah's house. Looking over, I'm caught off guard. A silhouette of a man standing before the gates catches my attention. Squinting, I can't make the person out. It's probably *him*, fucking psychopath.

Taken aback, I bring my focus back to the road and pull into Nathaniel's.

A client who loves to be degraded came in today. He is one of my favorites. No limits. We have a safe word should we ever find that limit one day, but it's been two years and he keeps coming back. With my long nails, my fingers squeezed his cheeks as I reminded him what a vile piece of shit he was while I allowed him to fiddle with his tiny penis. It's actually average size, but that is just a taste of what our sessions are like.

It makes me wonder how far Nathaniel will let me take it before he starts to fight back.

Chuckling to myself at the thought of him, this strong, powerful man at my mercy, his body shaking, begging for release while I edge him to the brink, makes my skin shiver in delight.

If he wants to keep this bullshit arrangement, he will get on his knees and suck my clit, like a good fucking boy.

Parking my car, I reach for my bag and get out. Wearing a black latex long-sleeved bodysuit, paired with a matching skintight knee-length skirt with a slit up the front, and my red soles, I head inside. I don't waste time by knocking, instead entering like I own the place. Which it will feel like for him soon enough.

With my head held high and my body walking with purpose, I make my way through the front entrance and down the hall toward his office, but I'm stopped just before I get there.

"This is my boyfriend, Darian Delacroix. I believe you met him the day my dick was hanging out of a hole in the wall. I hope you don't mind him joining this evening?" He pauses for effect, but I couldn't care less. "But don't tell his wife."

Before Nathaniel is able to continue with his lackluster joke, his bitch Delicroux pipes up. "Not a fucking chance."

Nathaniel smirks. "That is not what you were saying back in college."

Delicroux looks at me, mortified. "Never happened."

But Sinclair doesn't stop there. "And our slumber parties," he adds.

His friend has had enough. Waving his hands in the air, he walks away and mumbles, "He's talking out of his ass," before leaving.

Crossing my arms over my chest, my bag hangs off one, and I take Nathaniel in. My pussy tingles as my back stings. He is wearing fitted slacks and a shirt; his tie is discarded, and buttons are undone, revealing his chest. The white sleeves of his dress shirt are rolled up, exposing strong, tattooed forearms. The silver fox is groomed immaculately, wearing gold wire-framed glasses and black boots.

"What's in the bag, Ms. Vandenberg?" his deep, husky, and seductive voice questions.

Without missing a beat, I respond, "Your office, and I'll show you."

The silver fox steps to the side and holds a hand out, allowing me to lead the way, which I prefer. Adding a sway to my hips, I tease him, slowly sashaying past and leaving him behind as I turn into his space. My backside burns as I feel his eyes watching me.

I hate how much I like it.

His footsteps follow. And by the time he has joined me, I am sat on top of his large desk, legs crossed, and hands resting on either side of me.

"Please, Ms. Vandenberg, make yourself at home," he insists sarcastically.

Not allowing him to get in my head, I take him in once more, from his silver hair to his thin lips and strong chest. My eyes graze past his cock, and by the time I reach his feet, my words are spoken. "On your knees, Duke. We play by my fucking rules, if we play at all."

7

NATHANIEL

Her nipples are perk, as the latex glistens beneath the dim lights of my office. Wrapping my fingers around the thin wire of my glasses, I slowly remove them from my face while keeping eye contact with the devil before me.

Fiddling with the cool metal between my thumb and forefinger, I take two calculated steps toward her. She remains the same, pouty lips with red lipstick once again. Dark eye makeup with her signature slicked-back pony.

Rylee watches me with curiosity. What will I do next?

Without moving my gaze, I toss my glasses onto the brown leather couch to the side of me and take one last slow step. I can feel her warm, even breath on my skin.

If I were to tilt my head farther down, our noses would touch and our lips would brush.

I resist.

My hands adjust my trousers, my cock hard and pushing against the zipper, and my lips meet her ear. Before speaking, my nose takes in her sweet scent. Intoxicating.

"As you wish, Ms. Vandenberg," I whisper.

Rylee's body jolts ever so slightly. She's betting I didn't notice. But it's my job to notice everything.

Bending my knees and slowly making my way to the hard floor, I can feel her eyes on me the entire time.

I focus on her.

Bare pale legs crossed at the knee. Black pointed shoes with the red soles remain still. My eyes pass them, and I know, at any point, she could take my vulnerability and use it against me. One swift movement and she could take out my sight.

But she doesn't.

Fuck, the things I would do to run my fingers up her soft thighs. But I resist, allowing her to take the lead. My knees hit the floor, and my body gently folds, my backside resting on my legs while I wait for her next instruction.

"I know this is not something you are familiar with, Duke." Her voice is calm yet authoritative. And her statement is absolutely correct. I submit to no one;

they submit to me. But not for even a second did I question obeying her every demand.

"This may not be my dungeon, but we are still going to play by my rules." Her face is hard, and her eyes look into mine, trying to penetrate through the thick walls I've built around myself. She leans forward slightly as she speaks, each word carefully curated. "Mistress is what I demand. Ms. Vandenberg is what I'll accept only from you. Only during our sessions. Rylee is what you'll call me otherwise. Understood?"

I give a curt nod in understanding, but it's not good enough.

"I can't hear you."

Clearing my throat, my heart is racing, and I feel like a nervous schoolboy in the principal's office. "Yes, Ms. Vandenberg."

She smirks, satisfied by my response.

Uncrossing her long, delicious legs, the sole of her shoe placed on my forehead, she applies pressure, almost enough to push me back, but I resist, staying still.

"And you are not Duke in here, Mr. Sinclair."

Again, I accept these terms. She could tell me to put on a cloth diaper and cry like a baby, and I fear I would. She has me absolutely captivated; no fear or hesitation is sensed. She's strong, confident, and sees no limitations before her.

My heart continues to race; her head tilts. "Safe word, choose one."

"Greta," I say, chuckling to myself, but it does not impress her. The force of her foot gets stronger.

"Try again," she demands.

Apologizing, I pick a new one. "Right, sorry." Feeling the pressure, my mind races when the perfect word comes to me, one I know I'll never forget. "Devil."

Ms. Vandenberg rolls her eyes at me but releases some of the pressure of her shoe against my forehead, a sign she must be satisfied with my response. No praise leaves her lips.

It leaves me needy.

A million and one thoughts are circulating throughout my brain. I don't feel pressure, I don't panic, and I never show my hand.

And tonight, I broke every single fucking rule I have. Why? Because of the feeling I get when I'm around her. A feeling I never allow to enter my inner core with anyone else, not even my late ex-wife.

"It was you at Hell Fire Night, in the latex mask, wasn't it?" I suspect I already know the answer, but I need her verbal confirmation.

Her brows rise. Acknowledging me, a soft whisper follows, "Yes."

Our eyes locked at the cabin. I couldn't understand why, but I knew I needed to know more.

She isn't one to partake in Exiled traditions; I would have recognized her if she had.

It finally clicked when her dark eyes were looking up at me through her full lashes and my cock in her mouth; it was her. And now it's confirmed.

"If I may interject..." Before I am able to finish, I'm cut off.

"You may not."

I'm taken aback; my nostrils flare ever so slightly, and through gritted teeth I acknowledge her. "As you wish, Ms. Vandenberg."

Her foot leaves my skin, then both are placed on the ground before me, where I am still kneeled, at her mercy. Her bottom slides off the desk ever so slowly, and my mouth is watering with my cock still firmly pressing against my trousers.

With both hands on her hips, she says, "Playtime is over."

My heart drops. "The fuck it is. I paid..." Again, she cuts me off.

"Did you not understand the words that came out of my mouth, Mr. Sinclair? Or shall I repeat them for you?"

Swallowing my pride, for reasons of curiosity and the need to please her, I reply, "I understand, Ms. Vandenberg."

She walks past me, but I can feel her presence

behind me. "I could kill you right here, right now, if I wanted to." The venomous threat echoes in my ear.

"But you won't, or you already would have."

Rylee is quick to respond. "Perhaps I'm playing the long game, Duke."

Smirking, I say, "Good, that's exactly how I would do it too, Ms. Vandenberg."

She doesn't move from behind me, pondering my final words to her empty threat. Rylee already has me on my knees, at her mercy, while she has complete control. This is a reaction to something. But what?

I'll need to follow up with Rogers on her background check. I need to know everything.

My cell phone rings in my pocket, breaking the tension. Immediately, I am on my feet, reaching for it. The caller ID says things are not fucking good. "What?" I shout as I answer.

"He took her. She's gone!" is screamed at me, and my hard-on and desire to tongue fuck Rylee has evaporated for now.

"Send me the pin. I'm on my way."

Spinning around, I find Rylee is standing before me as Rogers comes running in.

Looking at him, I say, "I know. Rylee, do not fucking leave here. Do you understand?" My voice is stern.

She laughs. "The fuck I'm not."

I don't have time for this shit.

"Rylee. Greta said it herself. You're not to leave here. It's not fucking safe. Rogers, take her to one of the guest suites. No one in or out unless it's Elijah or me. Rain will be okay; he will have her in their panic room. I'm the fucking boss now. Do as you're told."

The laughter has stopped, confusion and concern has replaced it, and I don't have time to address either. Grabbing my glasses off the couch, I dial Elijah next. "Two minutes, be ready." As I hang up, I'm already down the hall with the front door in sight.

My fingers comb through my hair.

Here we fucking go.

8

NATHANIEL

I've called Delicroux a handful of times on the way to the abandoned warehouse.

D took off without me, fury and rage filling his eyes because they have his wife. We found out her location after my best friend took it upon himself to kidnap and torture former allies until someone finally revealed where she was.

His head isn't clear; we need a fucking plan. My hands bang against the dark leather steering wheel of his Bugatti in frustration.

I took his car. It's fast, and I like it.

We've officially drawn the line in the sand. Sides picked, and I feel no regret or remorse over it. I've spent my entire life devoted to an organization because that's what was expected of me. We are more powerful together than alone, my father would say. So, my blinders went on. I accepted my fate and gave myself to The Exiled. I went to law school for them so I was equipped for my role, which my father held prior, his father and his father's father. A role I was prepared to have die with me.

Elijah doesn't conform to others' ideologies. He kills. He will do it for anyone at any time if they allow him complete freedom to play. And I never fought it.

Never did I expect it to go down like this.

A war.

The King has done terrible things to Delacroix and Cecilia. Things all out of spite because he married what was promised to the King's son, Dalton.

Or has this been Dalton all along, as I've suspected?

And recently, my best friend was held up in the hospital because of them.

We have always known about rebel groups trying to destroy The Exiled and all the work we've done. I've always dismissed them. Ignored any reasoning they've tried to project on why we are "evil."

Since Cecilia, though, I get it. The Antichrist has presented hard evidence that cannot be ignored. Hell Fire Night has always been sold as a rite of passage, an initiation for the upcoming generation.

But it's all for show.

Brad, the King, and his merry men wanted the purest bloodlines taking over. Killing those in their way. And *those* people being our own members. Fellow Dukes and Duchesses, parents of the children who would one day initiate.

Children were left orphaned. For the sake of purity.

Those children include my brother by choice D and his wife.

Dalton is Cecilia's cousin.

Speaking of, my eyes widen with excitement; his car is within sight.

I slam down on the accelerator in order to pass him, and as I do, I grip the handbrake and pull it. The car spins, and my tires squeal against the hard pavement as the car turns sharply to cut him off. He brakes just before the front end of his vehicle crushes the side of the Bugatti I've borrowed.

I follow, stopping but not getting out. Instead, I observe his tantrum.

D's face is bright red as his chest heaves. He is yelling, but I tend to tune out my dear friend when he's entered this state. Waving at him politely, I tell him, "I think I'll stay right here, thank you," knowing I'm only agitating him further.

Storming off, he isn't missing for long.

Nope, he comes back even more pissed. How exciting, he has his gun pointed at me. "Get out of the car, Sinclair," he shouts like it's an added scare tactic to make me obey him.

Chuckling to myself, he can be so dramatic. I wait

briefly just to see how far he will go. Looking over once more, his eyes are bulging out of his head.

Best get to it then.

Opening the door, I get out. I grab my suit jacket on the way and stand; I adjust it and my slacks before walking around the car. My smirk remains. It keeps me from bursting out in laughter.

Leisurely, I come to stand before him. He's like a ravaged animal.

Down boy.

"What good are you to your woman if you're dead?"

He isn't amused by my question. He is acting on impulse, not logic.

"We are nearly there. What is wrong with you?"

"I've always admired you for being strategic. But when are you going to use some common fucking sense?" I throw back at him. At the same time, I'm stepping closer to him. Before I'm able to finish speaking, I'm on D, trying to disarm him. As I swipe his pistol, he stumbles to the ground from being completely caught off guard.

Before I can slap him around a little, a vibration goes off in my pocket. Jumping to my feet, I don't bother assisting Delacroix up. I'll let him wallow a moment longer. As I see the message on my phone, my heart drops and my face pales. I can feel my body slouch forward as I watch in disbelief.

Graphic photos and videos of Cecilia are staring

back at me. She's naked, bloodied, and bruised with a message informing me,

UNKNOWN

Times Up.

The fuck it is.

Faintly you can see she's encaged like a goddamn animal.

D can never see this.

"Where's your phone?" I ask as he brushes the dust off his pants.

Looking at me, confused, I catch a glimpse of it on his passenger seat. Rushing past him, I push him down once more. Behind me I can hear vulgarities being shouted, but I don't care. He can't see this.

Opening the passenger side door, I snag his phone, dropping it to the ground, then stomping on it with my boot.

"Why the fuck did you do that for?"

Looking back over at him, I say, "I need your head in the game. Emotions aside, because there's no going back for us."

We are a mile away from the warehouse when an army of blacked-out Range Rovers approach and park around us. Elijah didn't wait for me before leaving

early, and as a door opens on one of the Rovers, he jumps out, wearing all black with his bat in hand.

That's my fucking boy.

Clasping my hands together, with my own gun tucked away in my holster harness, I walk over to Elijah, placing my hand on his shoulder and reaching for my phone with the other. Using my body as a shield, I make it seem like I'm talking to Elijah privately when I'm really showing him what was just sent to me.

"Understood," is all he responds with.

Emotions. Feelings. To give two fucks about anything, it isn't really in him.

The real motive for showing him is to amplify his hunger to kill. He gets the mission.

Shouting can be heard from behind me. "Let's move out."

The rest of the crew prepares, equipped with everything we need for the rescue.

A thick tree line surrounds the warehouse, and we all make our way over. Hiding behind the brush, we are sitting ducks. He could have this place rigged—one wrong move, dead.

With a few hand singles made, everyone moves out, staying in the shadows to the best of our abilities. Reaching the door, my son, the one-man A team, kicks it in, and it flies open.

"Yes, son. Well done," I praise with excitement,

knowing exactly how much he hates it. Elijah's body flinches as I follow behind him.

It's quiet and dark. Unsettling.

Following my son, I'm on alert, watching for any sudden movement. We don't make it far before a body is seen on the floor—a commoner from Cecilia's protective detail. Shit.

D is the first to act. Crouching down, he tears the stapled note off the bloodied shirt.

Darian, enjoy your gift.

He passes it off to me, but I don't care to have possession of it and let it flutter to the ground.

Elijah walks farther in, looking for any sign of Cecilia or Dalton and his crew. But I can't shake the feeling that something is really fucking off. Then, in that exact moment, a droplet of red splatters onto D's shoulder. We both look at each other, confused, as another drops.

Looking up, I'm lost for words.

Seconds feel like minutes.

My brain finally registers what my eyes see.

"Holy mother of God." I'm horrified.

Chaos ensues, and a member of the team yells, "Someone get something to bring her down, NOW!"

Cecilia's hair hangs down toward us. Her body,

naked, battered, and bruised, is hung upside down from the rafters, attached to a cross.

Then, all at once, time speeds up, bodies are racing around me, and my mind and vision become focused.

"Elijah! Search the place. If any of *his* men have been left behind, interrogate, then kill. Understood?" I shout at my son, who, for once, looks shocked at the scene before him.

He nods then takes off, bat swinging while whistling a tune.

Cecilia is lowered, D is bent down, broken, and looking for any sign of life. It doesn't look good as her head rolls to the side. I crouch next to him, moving her blonde hair away from her face. "I'm so sorry." There is no way she's alive.

Darian rises and finds the commoner, who is still lying unconscious on the floor. Rage is released as loud roars echo. No one stops my best friend as he beats the commoner to death. Kicking him relentlessly, then moving to his skull. By the time he is done, brain matter is splattered all around.

Elijah comes back and takes in the destruction, looking over to D, and casually says, "Use the heel of your boot next time, gets it done quicker."

Only my fucking kid.

I move my fingers to check for a pulse one last time before I stand. I stop breathing and wait, pressing down firmly on her neck.

No.

"We have a pulse!" I yell in shock. "She's alive."

Paramedics are already rushing in. Darian races over and joins them as they take her out on the gurney.

I stay behind with Elijah and the others Greta sent from the Antichrist.

"I found something over here, Dad," Elijah says, grabbing my attention.

Nodding, I follow him as he leads, but before I see it, he points to the wall with his bat—*KING* is written in blood on one of the warehouse walls, with Cecilia's blood, I presume.

"Brad has to be dead. This motherfucker is getting his dick hard taunting us."

Since Darian and Cecilia married, we've been Dalton's number one target. His dad promised her to his son. Which is why my gut is saying he killed his dad. A false promise. Dalton has an ego and a hot head. Has always been reactive and hard to contain.

And since Darian married, it appears his missus has been associated with the rebel group, the Antichrist, who lives to take The Exiled down. Which, by default, we have gotten to know better. Dalton's taken notice.

Where D goes, I go. So when I say we, I fucking mean it.

Thomas rushes over to me, his face looking frantic. "Duke. I've just received word that Dalton appointed a new chief of police. One of his own men."

Keeping calm, I absorb what he's just told me and try to put together all the pieces. What is this little shit up to? He has completely broken protocol. I appoint chiefs and judges; the Sinclairs have been responsible for this for half a century. For as long as The Exiled has been in existence.

Dalton is now publicly declaring war on his own people. Perhaps he didn't like how we covered up the murder at the cabin; was that meant to be his public display as well?

This could ruin everything we have worked toward and invite worry and fear within the townspeople, but he's too high on power to realize the reality of the situation.

Smirking, I rub my hands together.

Elijah begins laughing.

Thomas is confused, too innocent to realize what's going through our heads.

We will fucking destroy his prepubescent army of assholes. This motherfucker doesn't stand a chance. We won't make a show of it. He won't see it coming. Just when all seems safe is when you should be the most scared.

Pulling my phone out, I dial Rogers and put it on speakerphone. "Everything we know on my desk by sunrise. Do you fucking hear me?"

His response is immediate. "Absolutely, Duke."

My mind flashes back to Rylee, who's still at my house. The Antichrist had been hiding and taking care of Cecilia, hoping Dalton got bored and hopefully moved on.

I'm positive Rylee knows nothing about the side hustle her grandmother operates. She seemed far too confused earlier when I mentioned Greta's instruction to stay put.

"Make sure Greta is present," I add before hanging up.

Looking out the window of Cecilia's hospital room, I let out a deep sigh and rest my hands in my trouser pockets. Cecilia is in rough shape, dehydrated, and covered in lacerations. Bruises are prominent on her face, and her blonde hair is stained in red, but she is going to be okay.

D comes to stand next to me and mumbles something barely audible. He's exhausted. Dark circles surround his eyes, and sadness fills the lines on his face.

I don't respond or ask for him to repeat himself. I'm not nervous about what I'm about to say, but concerned he is too tired to fully understand the implications of those words.

My breathing becomes heavier.

I can see Cecilia sleeping in the hospital bed in the reflection of the glass. Rage is coursing through my body. She's collateral damage to decisions we've made as members of The Exiled.

But my decision is made.

"Let's kill the King."

9

NATHANIEL

The sun is rising as I pull D's Bugatti into my driveway. Regardless of the events of the last twelve hours, I didn't care to give the car back yet.

Passing Elijah's, I notice his vehicle is still gone. He and Thomas were whispering about something before I left the warehouse for the hospital. I'm not sure Thomas is ready for Elijah, but it doesn't seem like he has a choice now.

A warm feeling fills my chest—it's pride. Has my son made a friend?

Besides Rain, Elijah hasn't cared enough to let anyone in. My excitement could be premature; Thomas still has time to become pig food, but I'm hopeful. Elijah is changing. And I get to witness it.

My eyes begin to well, but I shake it off. I'm exhausted, but the day is only beginning. I'll cry later, in the shower, where there aren't any witnesses. Cameras surround the compound, and Rogers is likely watching the feed.

Climbing out of the car, the fresh morning air dances on my skin. Inhaling deeply, it reinvigorates me. The exhaustion I felt moments ago washes away. A cool breeze follows, sneaking underneath my opened dress shirt. Taking my glasses off briefly, I squeeze the bridge of my nose before placing them back on my face and walk inside.

"Rogers! Coffee and food. I'm going to need all the fuel I can get today, old man," I shout into the foyer.

Tiny footsteps pull my attention to the second-floor banister.

Rylee looks disheveled, her hair a mess, and wearing one of my gray tees, which is like a dress on her. With tired eyes, she looks down at me. I'm pleased she's still here.

Perhaps more than I should be. But my feelings don't matter right now.

Clearing my throat, my voice is scratchy. "Everything is going to be okay. But first the earth will crack open and the fire of hell will escape. You will need your rest. Please, I insist you go rest your eyes while you can." Rylee's head tilts slightly at my cryptic statement, shaking her head in confusion, but she listens and walks back toward her room. My eyes linger on her petite, pale legs until they disappear down the hall.

Once she's gone, I look down at my ticking gold watch. They will be here any minute; I must prepare.

Greta was first to arrive, with a lit cigarette hanging out of her mouth. She didn't make a fuss, not wanting to alarm her granddaughter of her arrival. Another reason why I know Rylee doesn't know shit about the Antichrist.

Elijah had the opposite approach, with his bat dragging along the floor behind him and followed by Rain and Thomas.

D will be joining on speaker phone as he isn't leaving Cecilia's side at the hospital, and I don't blame him.

Rogers is last to enter, closing the door behind him. This is a need-to-know meeting, inner circle only.

And right now, I could go off. Absolutely crucify whoever was directly responsible for watching Cecilia, but we can't turn against each other now by playing the blame game. We have to be united. And I know Greta can handle her crew internally. They will suffer because this mistake is unforgivable.

My feet are resting on the hardwood desk, and the first thing I say wakes everyone up. "We are killing the King."

An awkward silence fills my office.

My eyes shift, wondering if the words I said weren't actually spoken out loud, so I repeat myself. "We are killing the King."

Greta pipes up. "We heard you the first fucking time."

Rain giggles into her hand. She keeps it real among all this seriousness.

"Hm, yes, Duke. We have some new intelligence since the events of last evening," Rogers stammers. I look at him, waiting for him to continue. Instead, he begins rummaging through his folder, pulling out one piece of paper and approaching me with it.

I take it, and at the same time Greta asks, "Which King are you talking about? Because that one is very fucking dead."

It's Brad's property.

At the end of his driveway, before the large gate, is a wooden stake, and on top of it is Brad's head.

Confirmed. Brad is dead. Dalton and his crew of merry imbeciles are likely responsible.

"The new self-declared one, Dalton," I say, unamused.

Rogers interjects, "Darian, the photo should be to you now."

D grunts, his way of saying, *Thank you.*

"They know we are connected to the Antichrist now. There's no going back. We have to be strategic— no room for error. Greta, you and your team are officially a massive fucking target." They were before, but it's elevated now that he knows D and I are officially with them.

"He will try and hit you where it hurts. Protect yourself and your people at all costs. Whatever you need, my resources are at your disposal." I pause as she nods in understanding, then continue. "And with the new chief of police appointed, it's hard to say what that pile of incompetence is capable of. They are unhinged and unpredictable. Look what they did to Cecilia!" I shout, slamming my fist down, pounding on my desk. My blood is boiling as images of her body hanging on that cross flash across my vision.

I then see Thomas startle from the corner of my eye. Elijah is smiling, sharp canines bared, begging to be released into the wild to play.

Looking at my son, I say, "We can't just attack them. They expect us to retaliate, and we will lose if we do. Instead, we wait. Lure them to us. Doing nothing will only infuriate them, causing a reaction. They will assume we are sitting fucking ducks again. We aren't. We will

simply be more deadly when they come to our house. Elijah, work with our men; discreetly prepare the compound and any other of our trusted properties. They could be watching, so we need to act as normal as possible. I'll give Ryder and his crew a heads-up.

Maybe work out a deal in case we need reinforcements."

Closing my eyes, I take a breath in. "We must never show weakness. If there's one thing I know, weakness is a delicious meal that people like me and people like him feed on."

Elijah wastes no time. Rising, he barks, "Thomas, come."

I look toward Rain, who is looking back at me, mouthing, "Oh my God," while silently chuckling.

"Don't worry, E, I'll be fine here," Rain jokes sarcastically. A language my son doesn't get.

His head rapidly turns at the sound of her voice. His expression is confused as he replies, "I know."

Thomas, who is standing at attention, follows Elijah out.

"Rogers, anything suspicious, you tell me immediately," I demand.

"Understood, Duke." Rogers is next to leave. He has connections all over this town. Money and promises talk. He is also excellent at cyber security, so perhaps blackmail also plays a small part in his little bird's loyalty.

Greta rises, not bothered that Rain is still with us, but she hangs my phone up on D before speaking further. "Nathaniel, keep her here. Please. Keep her safe." Greta reaches her hand out, placing it on my forearm in comfort. She's scared. I've never seen this side of her before.

I place my hand on top of hers. "I swear it. But you have to tell her."

It's not an ultimatum; it's her right. I'd keep her safe regardless, but she deserves to know.

"I'll do it this evening," Greta promises, squeezing my arm in reassurance before following the others out.

"You look exhausted. Shower. Rest. I may need your help with Thomas's body later. I can't see Elijah tolerating him long-term," Rain jokes as she stands on her feet. I laugh. But I think we both secretly hope it's not true.

The door closes behind her. I'm alone. At last.

Silence.

10

RYLEE

Steam surrounds me as hot water trickles down my body. Shampoo is lathered into my hair, smelling of mint and eucalyptus. As it rinses down my back, tiny stings can be felt from the fresh lacerations on my body. I tense but don't allow my face to react. It's part of my punishment still, until it scabs over and heals.

I follow with conditioner, which has the same aromatherapeutic scent.

He is a man who projects a strong image but requires balance. Each tiny detail in his home and behind the wall he's internally built shows me that.

A breeze of cool air overcomes the steam, followed by the overwhelming sensation of someone watching me.

He is here.

I don't turn or make it obvious that I'm aware of his presence. He is still a man in an organization that I detest. They ruin families. They ruin kind, good people, all for The Exiled.

Turning the water off, I reach for the towel and wrap it around my body. The shower is massive, lined with heated tiles, glass walls, and even equipped with a bench. A window is set in the middle with a view of the backyard and woods, mountains beautifully sitting behind. It never gets old.

Opening the shower door, the steam escapes and once it's all cleared, the view of him is clear.

A hand on the white granite countertop, legs crossed at the ankle, and still in the suit he had on last night. His gray hair is disheveled, eyes tired behind the wire frames, and his beard is in desperate need of tending to.

"Do you often watch houseguests in the shower?" Sarcasm is like a second language to me.

The corner of his mouth quirks up. "You are in my shower, so I don't see the issue."

He isn't wrong.

As the door closed to his office, I decided it was time to nose around. I found myself in his master suite, then naked in his bathroom, and decided it was a far better option than the smaller bath in my room.

Wringing out my hair, water drips onto the floor. His expression doesn't change. Still amused by my antics like I'm a child. His lack of response only further annoys me.

So, still ignoring him, I spin on my toes to leave and scurry back to my room to change, but his hand grabs my arm before I can.

"Who did that to you?" Nathaniel's voice is deep and eerie.

Fuck. My back.

"No one. It's nothing," I respond casually, not wanting to get into it.

"It's not nothing. Who? Names. Now!"

I'm not a coward; I own who I am and what I do. "Me. I did it," I confess confidently.

"Don't lie to me," he counters.

I shake him off, crossing my arms and turning around. My eyes narrow as I glare. "I'm not a liar. And don't act like you fucking care."

Nathaniel's face is stone, and through gritted teeth, he says, "I do care. Now, explain!"

My eyes roll, a habit I'm not ashamed of. "Not that it is any of your fucking business, because it's not. But if you must know, I broke my own rules by coming on your floor the other night. Remember, it was when I was on my knees sucking your cock?"

His nostrils flare; it seems like he is displeased by my answer, but I'm not here to tell him what he wants to hear.

Not wanting to continue with this conversation, I change the subject. "How old are you?"

Shaking his head, he throws back at me, "Does it matter?"

Tapping my chin with my finger, I reply, "Perhaps it does. Do you happen to have a life insurance policy with my name on it?"

"Well played, Ms. Vandenberg." He chuckles as his eyes glance over to the Mason jar I left on the counter.

Then curiously, he asks, "Who gave you that?" His head nods toward it.

"Thomas."

Then I remind him, as I take a step forward to grab my juice, "We aren't in a session. Rylee is what you will call me."

Nathaniel blows out a deep sigh and shakes his head. "My apologies. But I'll need you to leave that here."

I'm agitated now. "No. He said it was fresh green juice," I respond in defiance. I will never have a man tell me what I'm allowed to eat or drink.

Unscrewing the tin lid, he brings the glass jar to his nose and smells it, then places it back down. Squeezing the bridge of his nose, Nathaniel then informs me, "It's poison."

Why would Thomas try to poison me?

My face apparently says it all.

"It seems like my son doesn't care for your presence

here. But don't mind him; it's harmless. He knew I would stop you from having it."

Perplexed, I question, "Thomas is yours too?"

"No. Thomas is who Elijah had deliver you this cocktail. Thomas likely had no idea what was inside. See, harmless," Nathaniel reassures me casually, but I don't feel reassured at all.

I don't respond to any of it.

Elijah is a member of The Exiled.

Is he trying to do to me what they did to my mom?

I turn and start walking away from my host, my heart racing alongside my mind.

Before I am able to fully escape his presence, he shouts behind me, "Greta needs to speak to you. It's important."

I stop, caught off guard by his statement.

He and my grandmother are closer than I care for. This is the second time he's mentioned her, and I don't like it.

WALKING DOWN THE STAIRCASE, the house is quiet. Nathaniel's bedroom door is closed. I had a message from Greta waiting on my phone after my shower. He was right; she wants to talk and will be over later this evening.

I feel unsettled.

Clothes were waiting for me in the dresser, leggings and an oversized tee. My hair hangs long over my shoulders, still damp.

Rogers pokes his head out from the hall. "I've sent someone for your belongings; they should be here shortly." He then disappears.

Nathaniel is going to pay for this later.

Roaming around, I find myself in the kitchen. A fresh pot of coffee is calling my name with a mug sitting next to it. I pour myself a cup and drink it immediately. I love it hot, like burning tongue hot.

With my coffee in hand, I walk back upstairs, as another closed-door room had piqued my interest from earlier.

Standing before it, my hand reaches toward the cool metal doorknob. Turning it, I can tell it's not locked now as the knob allows me to rotate it fully around.

Pushing the door open, the room is dark with a sliver of light peeking through the curtains. It's also dusty and aged. Flicking the light on, a couple pictures are hung that look like a child has drawn them. Stepping onto the carpeted floor, I take another sip of my coffee as I examine the drawings. A little boy with a bat —this must be Elijah's childhood room. The space is sparse, shelves without clutter. The bed is made, and the dresser is bare.

"Get. Out."

The words startle me.

Slowly, I turn. A man with a skeleton face stares back at me. His wooden baseball bat is pointed at me, dented and bloodstained.

Elijah Sinclair.

"Shocked I'm still alive?" I ask.

His face shows no emotion, no anger, or annoyance. Just straight-up uncaring.

"Unfazed. Plenty of other ways to kill you," he says.

Lovely. I suspect winning father of the year awards won't be in his future.

Taking another sip of my coffee, I'm apprehensive but inquire against my better judgement, "Why do you want me dead?"

"I don't trust you."

I've heard he only tolerates his father and partner, Rain, so his response isn't alarming. I'm also grateful he doesn't acknowledge my distaste for The Exiled, which means my plan to destroy his father is still a secret safe with me.

Elijah impatiently repeats himself. "Get the fuck out of my room."

I bow to him, sarcastically. "As you wish, Prince."

But I need to be careful; having him focused on me adds another obstacle to my plan that I don't need.

11

NATHANIEL

He is taunting me. Letting me know he's watching. Or just guessing and trying to make me paranoid. Regardless, he is dangerous.

But as they say, defense wins championships, and I plan on fucking owning him by the end of this. Deadman Dalton. I chuckle at the nickname I've gifted him.

I've been able to catch a couple hours of sleep, but those marks on her back haunted my dreams. They are all I see each time I blink.

She hurts herself. On purpose. But why? Those wounds were fresh, so I know she wasn't lying. But I need to understand.

Looking at the time, Greta should be over in the next hour or so. I move to get out of bed when my bedroom door swings open. Looking over, it's Rylee.

And she's pissed.

Her lips are pursed and her eyes narrow.

I'm excited.

"You have people gathering my belongings?"

My dick hardens from her tone. Seething with venom, just how I like her.

"Yes, please come in." I jokingly wave her in as I adjust my hard cock before rising.

"Sit down," she demands, and I obey without hesitation. My heart begins to race in anticipation. What's next?

"You are a man who is used to calling the shots. Getting his way and having no one to answer to but yourself. Those days are over. Do you understand me?" Rylee steps toward me, hands placed firmly on her hips, and each word spoken is clear, unrushed, and concise.

My eyes move down. I go from looking at this strong woman to my bare, tattooed feet on the ground. My words come out, hushed. "It feels good. Not being in control. It is a break for my brain. To just live and be.

To listen to someone else. You have no idea how desperately I needed this..."

It's the truth.

Even if it is only for thirty seconds, it's those seconds my brain isn't always playing chess, trying to predict what's to come or has been and how to handle it.

Bending girls over my desk got me off, but it never fully satisfied me.

"Do you remember your safe word?"

Shifting eyes look at her. My body turns slowly to face her, and I nod. But Rylee isn't satisfied with my response. "Say it," she demands.

Clearing my throat, I say, "Devil."

The corner of her mouth rises. Satisfied, she steps closer, and her bare legs taunt me.

"Mr. Sinclair, I do hope your men get *all* my things. We could have a lovely time with them." Her face glows with excitement.

Fuck. So do I.

"On your back." Her voice firms, becoming more serious. Lifting my legs back onto my bed, her voice penetrates my ears once more. "I can't hear you."

Looking up at her, she glares.

"Yes, Ms. Vandenberg."

This warrants a "Good boy."

My cock twitches underneath my underwear at hearing it.

"You're lucky I found a treat from my dungeon in my overnight bag."

Rylee's fingers slowly glide up her thighs and disappear under the hem of her long shirt. She has something tucked away; I can briefly see something pushing against her shirt as it moves down her body.

A glint of light from outside hits it, bouncing off the silver object as it becomes uncovered.

"Take your cock out," she demands.

Taking a deep breath, my chest rises and my heart continues to race. Moving my hands to my abdomen, my fingers hook under my waistband, and I shimmy my underwear down. Arching my back, they slide under my backside and down my pelvis. My cock springs out, precum already leaking from my tip. As I continue to remove my boxer briefs, my balls are exposed next.

"Stop," she demands.

And I listen.

Removing my hands from the waistband, my palms sweat in anticipation. Her eyes remain unmoved, staring at my face, completely unfazed by my exposed cock. It is taking everything in me to not touch myself, to tug on him while rubbing my tip, desperate for release.

Fuck it.

My fingers wrap around my girth, squeezing my cock hard as I pull on him and take her in.

Then, in the blink of an eye, Rylee is on the bed. Her knees between my legs with a deadly scowl on her face. "I never said you could touch."

Letting go, I admit defeat. No point in arguing with her. She is in control. She speaks; I obey.

At the same time, that silver object is being placed around my cock, between two of my barbell piercings.

"What do you say?" Her brow arches in amusement.

"I'm sorry, Ms. Vandenberg." I'm always man enough to apologize and mean it.

The object tightens around me, and as it does, she informs me, "Bad boys don't get rewarded."

With each turn, I feel a sharpness poking my sensitive skin, like teeth but sharper during a blowjob.

I let a hiss out as my pelvis flexes, and my muscles tighten, causing my dick to move. The spikes nip it, stinging me as a quick sharp pain moves around me.

Once satisfied, her hands lift and grip my balls.

"Please, not my balls, Ms. Vandenberg," I plead. I don't think I can handle them being spiked like my cock. I'd cry on my knees, begging if it kept my balls safe.

"This is for touching yourself without permission. You will keep it on for the remainder of the day. Do you understand?"

My response is immediate—anything to protect my balls. "Yes, Ms. Vandenberg."

Leaning forward, her top hangs and skims my bare chest. Her lips are just inches from mine. I need to taste them, to taste her. Both sets.

Her scent is sweet, addictive, and torture.

Licking her lips, her tongue teases me, moving slowly. She then whispers, "Now, get up. Greta should be here shortly."

"Yes, Ms. Vandenberg."

Rylee's hand reaches up, gripping my chin as her thumb rubs along my manicured facial hair. My cock throbs, and the spikes pinch me yet again. Not wanting to seem like a pussy, I keep the pain hidden. But it's oddly satisfying.

The trust you have to have with one another in this situation has to be strong, and for two people who have barely spoken to each other, this is remarkable and intimate.

She has mentioned she could kill me at any moment. And she could. But I would fucking let her if it made her happy.

She is one of three people who can see right through me. But this is deeper than with the others. I wonder if she feels it.

Getting up, her scent leaves me first, then her touch. My hooded eyes watch as she leaves, closing the door behind her.

And this is the exact moment I realize, and she

knows it too. It would be impossible not to because I have no game face when it comes to her. No strategy. No racing thoughts or game play.

What is this woman doing to me?

12

RYLEE

Greta sits on the brown leather chair across from me. Nathaniel is sat wide-legged on his desk chair, the spiked cock ring making it impossible for him to cross his legs.

Her glittered walker rests before her, and shockingly, a lit cigarette isn't hanging between her lips.

"Shall we get to it then?" Nathaniel breaks the silence.

I'm sat back, legs tucked under me, as I wait in suspense. I feel like a little kid about to be told off by her parents as silence refills the space.

Greta takes a couple more deep breaths in. I've never seen her like this before, shook.

Nothing rattles her, and it turns my suspense into worry and fear.

"It's not safe for you at home. You can't come back."

I jump forward. This isn't about to happen. "I'm absolutely not staying here, if that's where you're going with this."

She holds her hand up to me. "Let me finish, dammit."

Her tone catches me off guard. Greta has told me off plenty, but this time hits differently. Unease further creeps up my body.

My grandmother leans forward, gathering a cigarette and lighter from her bag. "You need to listen when I speak. Don't interrupt me," she commands, lighting her cig and then leaning back.

A cloud of smoke fills the room as she exhales. "The King is dead. Dalton, that little shit, took advantage of Hell Fire Night. We have evidence that Brad was beheaded and was turned into an ornament at the end of his estate driveway.

"We must tread carefully. Change is upon us, and dark clouds are coming over our town. I will have the Antichrist keep an eye on you, but I need their main focus and energy elsewhere. You will never see them. You will never know who they are."

I don't let her finish before interjecting. "What the fuck are you talking about?"

Greta rolls her eyes at me. Frustrated, she points at me with her lit cig between her fingers. "Get to understanding. Because one day you will take it over. When I'm gone, everything becomes yours."

My head shakes in disbelief, and my childhood flashes before my eyes as I try to search for clues and understanding. Any signs that I missed that could have warned me about this. Instead, Greta continues. "I started the Antichrist when your mother died. And as each Hell Fire Night took place, it only continued to give us more of a reason to keep the organization going. Every five years, on Hell Fire Night, we rebel against it. Try to take The Exiled down and eliminate their existence, and end their night of murder and chaos. It has impacted our family, yes, but also their own members. It's barbaric."

The words slip out as I try and piece everything together. "Nathaniel is Exiled. Why are you telling me this in front of him?"

"He knows about us. He knows who I am and what I represent. The closest people to him have been lost because of their organization. Cecilia was our responsibility, then Darian wed her. Both have lost parents because of The Exiled. Nathaniel's family took Darian in and have been inseparable since. Thomas is also one of us. When that terrible event happened with Cecilia, it was decided. Nathaniel and Darian started working with us to take down the new dictator and his crew of idiots."

Nathaniel interrupts. "Wait a minute. Don't downplay what D and I have. Even if he wants to hide our cuddle parties from the world. It's magical."

Greta waves him off, and I try to hide my laugh. I know if his best friend were here now, he would be cringing. At the same time, out of habit, he goes to cross his legs. He winces and quickly readjusts to have his foot hanging off his knee, giving his cock enough space without the added pressure on the spikes.

What I would do to have it tug one of his barbells. I smile at the thought. The sensation is similar to teeth but sharper and scarier, mentally.

"Get out of your head. This is serious," Greta scolds, but before she is able to continue, a thought comes to me.

"Thomas tried to kill me. He isn't one of yours."

Similar to Nathaniel, she also waves me off. "Rylee, it was Elijah. Thomas had no idea what was in the Mason jar." My eyes widened in shock. Why is this not a big deal to anyone?

"It's safer for you here. Nathaniel and Elijah have more resources to protect you than I do. I can't lose you like we lost your mother." She's being vulnerable with me in front of others. Tears prick my eyes.

Pointing at Nathaniel, I state, "They are why Mom is gone. And you want me to stay with them?"

"It wasn't me. Or Darian. But I understand why you hate the idea and periodically mention the idea of killing me. I would too if I were in your position."

I cut him off. "You have no idea what it's like to be in my situation. They killed your best friend's parents, but you didn't even care. I bet you and your family forced him to initiate. So, no, you don't understand shit about anything." Then I look over to Greta. "And if I'm to take over, why not tell me before today? Why hide all of this from me my entire life?"

Her head falls back onto the chair, her voice hushed. "I was hoping this shit would be over by the time that happened." She is defeated, and it hurts my soul seeing her like this, but she's not done. "He found out she was pregnant with you. Five years passed since your birth. We never saw or heard from him. Until Hell Fire... He couldn't have her making any claims to the Kingdom of The Exiled, not with his own son just being born."

From the corner of my eye, I see Nathaniel burying his head in his hands.

Greta's eyes close, and she whispers, "Brad was your father. You were a result of a one-night stand... Dalton is your half-brother."

You could hear a pin drop alongside my heart.

"So, please, Rylee... I can't have you die by their hands." If she could get on her knees and beg, I guarantee she would be right now.

There is so much to process and take in. I have *their* blood in me. The blood of the people who have hurt so many fucking others. For what? A night of chaos? To hunt and kill without consequences? It seems like they never had any consequences to begin with.

"Brad killed your mother. Dalton has tried to and almost succeeded in killing your cousin, Cecilia. You cannot be risked." As Greta finishes, the magnitude of the situation hits me. If my grandmother is scared, then maybe I should be too.

Then, the door opens and Rogers enters. "Duke. Sorry to interrupt, but the police are at the gate. Claiming it's a wellness check."

NATHANIEL

"Hello, Chief Fredricks, couldn't get a judge to sign off on a warrant? Falsifying a wellness check to conduct a search must go against your police policies."

Three lit-up police cars are parked in front of my gate, and Chief Fredricks has his arms crossed over his puffed-out chest.

"Open the gate, Sinclair," he barks.

"I'd rather not," I toss back at him. I'm well within my rights to refuse him entry; he isn't stepping a foot on my property.

"We received a call that a female was being held here against her will. Let us come in, check on her, then leave. That's all I ask."

Snapping my fingers, I try to remember. "How does that Gwen Stefani song go again? This shit needs a warrant, W-A-R-R-A-N-T," I riddle, only further pissing Fredericks off.

I also have D on an open line acting as my attorney. "For fucks sake."

He is still at the hospital with Cecilia, and she won't be released for a few more days. Until then, her room is locked down, and he isn't leaving her side, rightfully so. It isn't safe for us anymore. A civil war has been declared, sides chosen, and only one can win. And I can fucking promise it will be our side.

"Get a warrant or proof of cause and we will gladly let you in. Until then, Chief, you will remain on the outside of Sinclair's gates," D interrupts my thoughts with his legalities. We went to Harvard together, both graduating with law degrees. As much as I joke around, I know my shit too, but it's never wise to represent yourself, so we often act as each other's council, when needed.

"Piggies need a snack." Fantastic, Elijah's here. I know he wants so desperately to play and soon he can, but now—now is not the fucking time to be trolling these assholes.

Then honking follows loudly from behind me. Greta.

The shitstorm keeps getting better. "Kindly move, so my guest can leave," I shout at the chief, who is still parked outside my gate.

"This isn't over, Sinclair," he hollers back.

I wave as he gets back into his car. "Looking forward to it."

13

RYLEE

I'm alone in my room, sitting on the edge of the bed with the lights off. The silence is tranquil while I reflect on the last couple of days.

Greta's never spoken about my birth father before. I had no idea… which makes me wonder, does Dalton? Things are too uneasy now to risk fleeing and going back to the comfort of my own room. Cecilia is still in the hospital, and I could end up in a casket, like my mom.

Tears well in my eyes. I blink once to give them the opportunity to escape down my cheeks. At first, this arrangement was an unexpected gift. I latched on to it so I could avenge my mother and kill The Exiled in their sleep under their own roofs.

Now what?

What is my purpose?

Someone knocks on my door, but I don't move or speak. It doesn't matter because the door gingerly opens, a sliver of light peeks through the crack, and a tall shadow appears. Nathaniel.

Clearing his throat, he asks, "May I?".

"It's your house," I answer curtly. It's rude. He hasn't done anything, but I don't know how else to act. I'm mad and frustrated, and... I don't know how to process this.

Then a thought occurs to me, I've been here for days and missed sessions. "What do my clients think?"

He is somber in response, likely as exhausted as I am, but his game face is better than mine. This is the life Nathaniel grew up in. "Greta told them you had a family emergency out of town."

Nodding, my gaze focuses before me.

"Did you know?" I know the answer but need to hear it from his mouth to my ears.

"Yes."

"When?"

He takes a single step forward. I can hear his fingers brushing through his hair, something I've noticed he does when he doesn't want to respond but has to. "I had Rogers do a workup on you after the first night you came here. Only you, me, D, and Greta know. And I'll make damn sure it stays that way, I swear it, Rylee." His voice is revealing. Pain and fear. He's being vulnerable in front of me again. A tactic or genuine, I'm not sure yet.

"I will keep you safe. He won't get to you," he promises.

My bloodline technically makes me Queen of The Exiled. I'm older than Dalton, barely, but it still puts me at risk. If he finds out, or already knows about our connection, I'm dead.

It's why Greta was so adamant about keeping me here.

"I know this isn't ideal, but nothing happens by accident. We are always where we should be." Nathaniel pauses before continuing. "I also know what I am about to ask is rather inappropriate, but could you please remove the spikes from around my cock? Walking bow-legged in front of the chief of police was rather uncomfortable."

I erupt with laughter—hysterical laughter. This situation is so incredibly fucked up that it's all I can do or feel right now.

"No. It's staying on," I respond between losing my mind. Nathaniel blows out a heavy breath of frustration.

"It's nipping. Please, Ms. Vandenberg?" My brow arches, and my laughter subsides.

"Doing as *you* please would be too easy. That's not how this works, Mr. Sinclair." I'm smug, but when we play, it's by my rules.

Standing, my chest is puffed out as confidence cascades over me. Still in my lounge clothes with my hair down, I reach for my hair tie sitting on my nightstand. Gathering my long locks, I pull it up into my signature high pony.

After returning to my room from meeting with Greta, I noticed a few more of my belongings had arrived. Tiptoeing to the leather duffle bag on the royal purple velvet sitting chair, I take the zipper between my fingers and deliberately, I open it slowly. It feels like the air is slowly being sucked out of the room as the teeth of the zipper unlatch and tension builds.

The bag opens and the items inside are revealed. My mouth smirks with excitement.

Shiny silver chains make my eyes glimmer—nipple clamps. Biting my lip, my hands reach in to see what else this mystery bag contains. And to my surprise, whoever packed this did me a great favor; lubricant and a few different-sized silver metal butt plugs with bejeweled rubber ducks on the ends follow, gifted from Greta. Some clothes are at the bottom, and a pair of black metal handcuffs are the last of it.

"You have thirty seconds to get on the bed. No clothes," I demand.

Expletives are mumbled under his breath that he will be disciplined for. As I keep my back facing him, I can hear his belt buckle jingling as he rushes to disrobe.

The bed squeaks, indicating that he is nearly how I want him. The cuffs are the first item I take. "Safe word?"

Breathlessly he answers, "Devil."

"Good boy, Mr. Sinclair," I praise while standing in place a few moments more because I can play mind games too, Nathaniel.

Without hesitation, my body turns and my eyes trace down his exposed, fit body. Black ink decorates every inch of his skin, with the exception of his cock. White hair lightly covers his chest, his nipples are erect, and his breathing is becoming more heavy. The spiked cock ring is still in place, adding to the allure of his dick alongside those piercings.

My pussy throbs and my mouth waters. Soon, girl, soon.

"Let's both not feel together, if only for a little while." My voice is husky, lust and desire dripping off each word, and I hate myself for it.

"Arms up, above your head," I instruct. His eyes close, debating if he will do it, perhaps? This is his last chance to flee before we begin. But he doesn't. Nathaniel's strong arms move up my bedsheets and as they do, I take another step forward. I am holding the cool metal cuffs with my index finger, mindlessly twirling them while I wait for him to get into position.

His piercing blue eyes stay on me; trust is important and he has given me his wholly. Laying vulnerable with many unknowns still to come isn't for everyone. You either get it or you don't, and I can feel his energy bouncing off mine; his yearning to let go, to be free, and to have me lead is admirable. Many men in his stature would never, but he trusts me to lead him, and I will never take this responsibility lightly.

My knee lifts to rest on the edge of the bed as I lean over his face. I take his wrist in my grip, leaving my thumb resting over his pulse that is racing as I cuff him. My fingers move up his hand once the cuff is locked into place. I brush the beds of my fingers over the gold rings adorning his fingers. I am nearly too captivated to notice the goosebumps rising on his skin from the brief but intimate moment.

Nathaniel only wears gold accessories; they complement his beauty and bring out his features. This man is majestic. On his other wrist is his gold watch. Reaching farther, I gently remove it and place it on the bedside table before locking his other wrist in.

"Keep your hands above your head. Don't move them unless I tell you to." I don't have any rope or other chains to connect to the bed frame and the cuffs to make it nearly impossible for movement.

"Understood, Ms. Vandenberg." I reward him with a smile, he is learning.

Kneeling next to him, my fingers curl around the hem of my shirt and I take it off in one quick movement, exposing myself to him. Time stills; a man has never looked at me the way he gazes at me. Nathaniel's eyes penetrate my soul. Lust and devotion radiate from him. And not because I am dominating him but because he genuinely feels that way. Energy never lies.

This is not the place nor time for me to even try to comprehend this.

"Many men are fixated on owning a woman. Many men think ownership includes penetrating all our holes. And I have always been an advocate for equal rights, Mr. Sinclair."

My silver fox freezes. Our moment is over as realization washes over him. "Unless this is a hard limit."

Swallowing, his Adam's apple bobs. From the corner of my eye, I see his toes flex as he contemplates his next words. "No, it's not, Ms. Vandenberg."

Turning around, I reach for the lube and smallest plug. This is likely his first time being anally penetrated, he needs to be trained to handle more before I even attempt to fit him with a larger size.

I lather the plug with lube and pour extra into my own hand. I walk to the end of the bed. "Knees up, cradle them toward your chest, and push your butt forward."

No words follow, he just obeys.

Sitting on the bed, I position myself between his raised legs. Nathaniel's cock bobs, still leaking precum, and my eyes attempt to hood at the sight, but I stop myself. Placing my hand to his hole, I begin coating his opening in the extra lube. I then take one finger and push it inside of him, rimming his entrance. He isn't used to the intrusion, immediately tensing up. "I need you to relax, it's just the tip of my index finger. I won't go any farther with it."

Nathaniel blows out a deep sigh as his muscles relax, allowing me to finish. Sliding my finger out, I look at his face. Beads of sweat are already forming along his hairline and his forehead, he is nervous.

Holding the plug up, he doesn't look at it, instead maintaining eye contact with me as I speak. "Stay just like this. I will gradually insert the plug only as your body adjusts to the size. I will never force it in, I will never intentionally make something painful unless it's for pleasure. Remember the safe word if you need."

Nathaniel doesn't object, therefore I proceed. My eyes admire the incredible man laying here before me, the dimples on his cheeks as his ass flexes with his abdomen.

I position my body on all fours, my mouth dangerously close to his cock, but I keep my eyes on where my occupied hand is. I place the tip of the silver plug at the entrance. "Relax," I coax softly. He does while blowing out a couple more breaths.

Millimeter by millimeter, I ease the cool silver plug inside of him. Anytime I see his face or body tense, I pause, allowing him time to adjust before proceeding. My hand is gripping the gem-encrusted rubber duck.

My fingers wrap around it, and I know it is all the way in once I feel his soft skin against mine.

"You're doing so good," I praise.

His breathing is now audible, like he just ran a marathon, and his words are shaky as he speaks. "Thank you, Ms. Vandenberg."

"Now, slowly lower your legs. You are going to feel full, uncomfortable, but your body will adjust."

Obeying, my silver fox does what I ask.

Next, I reach for the nipple clamps, my breasts are above his face, his breath warm against my skin while showing excellent restraint.

Sitting back on my legs, kneeling, I lean forward and blow my breath on his. My free hand plays with his chest hairs, and my nails scratch his skin, causing him to hiss. I attach the clamps, one to each nipple, the chain resting loosely on him as his back arches. As I lean back, resting my bottom on my legs, I notice Nathaniel is overwhelmed with sensations. His nerves are unfamiliar with them, causing his brain confusion on how to respond. Soon, it will tell him this is pleasure, not pain. Delicious and addictive pleasure.

Before I move to the next part, I remove my bottoms, leaving me completely exposed. He will see it as a level playing field, but I don't. I find it freeing.

Next, I add another level to our session, gripping his length just below where I placed the spiked cock ring and tug at it ever so slightly. Another hiss follows, and I smile in satisfaction.

My thumb finds the release, and I apply enough pressure that it unlatches, falling off him.

Nathaniel is flabbergasted as his arms move from above his head. "Wait, I could have just removed it myself?"

I am quick to respond, slapping his face—not hard, but with enough force that he feels the same sting that I do against my palm. Then, in rapid succession, I grip his chin and make eye contact. "Arms up and no speaking unless you are spoken to!" I remind him firmly as we remain in an intense stare-off. He is still very new to this, so I take it easy on him, but my pussy is dripping from his defiance. This shit gets me so horny. I smirk sadistically, knowing I get to put him right back in his place.

Time slows as I wait. He is testing me, seeing how serious I am or if I will back down. I won't. I've been living my best life for years.

He is the first to move; his cuffed wrists that are hanging in midair proceed to move back onto the bed over his head.

Such a good boy for me.

Keeping his cock in my hand, I sit up and position myself over him, taking his tip and circling my pussy with it. Nathaniel grunts, and it's music to my ears.

Teasing him more, I can hear our juices mixing. My

mouth waters as I position him at my opening and slowly slide down his length. The ridges of his piercings feel insatiable against the walls of my cunt. I grip myself around him, wanting to keep them close.

"You move, I stop. Do you understand?"

Nathaniel nods once. "Yes, Ms. Vandenberg."

And this time, I praise him out loud. "Good boy." Followed by a cheeky wink.

My pelvis moves and my back arches. Reaching behind me, I place my hands on the mattress, allowing his cock to rub me right where I need it.

"You feel so fucking good," I whimper. The buildup to this moment sends me spiraling. I have craved his cock since I first had it in my mouth, and I needed to feel it inside of me. And now that I have it, I will never let it go. Each barbell is massaging my pussy; his tip feels like it's halfway up my body. Nathaniel is the biggest I've ever had.

My movements quicken, my body is begging for release. Tonight, if he doesn't come by the time I do, he will be walking around with blue balls until I give him permission to unload.

The tingling starts at my toes. Repositioning myself, I reach in front of me, pulling at the chain hanging from each of the nipple clamps. Breathlessly, I ask, "Does it hurt?"

His head shakes. "No, it all feels so fucking good."

My lips quiver as my orgasm builds. "Open your

mouth," I demand, and with no time wasted, he does. Leaning forward, I spit the excess saliva accumulating in my mouth into his. At the same time, I tug the chain and the clamps follow, snapping his sensitive, hard nipples.

His body jolts while a sweet moan escapes.

My entire body is trembling; I have resisted my release for as long as I can.

"Come," I hiss out. Dropping the clamps next to me, I reach for the plug and rapidly dislodge it from him, making his orgasm even more intense.

I can feel his cum filling me as mine coats him.

Letting go of the plug, I reach up and pinch my nipples. The sweet sting feels so fucking good. My movements slow. Nathaniel's eyes are barely open and his breathing is heavy. I can feel sweat beading down my face with each aftershock that hits me, leaving me quivering on top of him. With shaking arms, I reach over him and unhook the cuffs. I nearly fall into him, resting on his chest, but I stop myself.

I gave in to this, sex, but this is as far as I'll go.

Then it occurs to me what we just did—we had sex. I gave in and also made it about my own desire and pleasure beyond what I normally do. There is no after-glow. I go into shock because of my own actions with a man who I should hate, but due to unforeseen circum-stances, I shouldn't?

Shaking my head, I ask, "Would you like water? A bath with salts?"

Aftercare is as important as our sessions.

Nathaniel's voice is hoarse. "No. Just sleep." I nod and slide off of him. His cum drips out of me and down my thighs. I leave it there, because I like it.

Our cum coats his glistening cock.

Sleep sounds incredible, and I am suddenly incredibly tired. Exhaustion sweeps over me; it's been building, but I've ignored all signs of it until now as I let a yawn escape me.

I don't bother cleaning myself up. Sliding under the soft blankets next to him, my eyes are heavy as my head hits the pillow. Nathaniel doesn't move. Giving in to the day, I close my eyes, leaving the world behind, if only for a few hours.

NATHANIEL

A loud shriek of terror wakes me. Throwing the blankets off me, I am already on high alert looking for the source.

It doesn't take me long. Rylee.

She is standing, wrapped in a throw blanket from the end of the bed, looking out the glass doors that open to the balcony overlooking the backyard. Racing up behind her, I look in the same direction she is and my face goes red as anger fills me.

My fist clenches and pounds on the glass, causing her to jump. Before I can comfort her, my brain needs to comprehend what exactly I am looking at. My eyes shift around my backyard in absolute disbelief.

Brad's head is at the center of it, on a wooden stake in the yard. His eyes have dried blood staining down his cheeks, his mouth sewn shut. Around him, various states of death are on display, from flesh to bones. Some are encased in wooden coffins with the lids open to hang out of an old car's trunk. A few are hanging from large tree branches, either from the throat or wrists.

Then a few truly throw me off. They are in sleeping bags, only their heads sticking out.

"ELIJAH!"

14

NATHANIEL

Standing in the front entrance of my son's house, I am fucking fuming. "Get your ass over here!" I shout and my voice echoes around me.

Rain is first to peek around the corner. "What did he do?" She already knows whatever it is has to be a new level of grotesque as I am yelling.

"Where is he?" I ask as I take in her new pregnant body. Rain's bump only popped a few days ago, and with each change, Elijah amps up his level of fuckery. It's how he copes, but fuck me, a body farm in my backyard?

"Out back with the pigs." She smirks. I am so grateful to have her in our family; she helps balance my boy and makes this family a little more loving than it had been previously. So I casually tell her why I am so pissed off while making my way to the back door. "Body farm. Brad's head is at the center of it."

Rain sighs. "He's been watching your house at night. Greta's granddaughter is absolutely on his radar. He knows there is something there without fully understanding it, if that makes sense? He doesn't know how to feel... about it." Her words cause me to pause.

"It's nothing. Just an arrangement of sorts."

I can feel her smirk and eye roll burning into the back of my head. I should know better than to bullshit her, but to be frank, I don't even understand what *this* is.

Stepping outside, I spot my target immediately and his new sidekick, Thomas.

"You little shits," is all I get out before I take a step forward into a giant pile of pig shit. The vile smell is activated as it clings to my clothes, shoes, and skin.

And ever so frankly, Elijah advises why I am ankle deep in it. "Fertilizer."

Pressing my lips together, I try to gather my composure. "Elijah. Son. I've always supported you. Been your cheerleader, for lack of better words. But, son..." I pause, shaking my foot free. "I need help understanding why you've made a body farm in my backyard."

Then he waves me off, like it's not a big fucking deal. "It will only smell in the summer. The cold weather should suppress a lot of the odors. I find it interesting to watch how bodies decompose, given different situations and positions within and on top of the earth."

"Why couldn't you do this at your house?" I shake my head in utter disbelief. Is this conversation even real? Or a figment of my imagination?

Twirling his bat and still not even looking in my direction, he replies, "I wanted too, but Rain went on about kids and inappropriate things for them to see. The kid isn't even born yet, it makes no fucking sense, Dad. Then I thought, wait, this could be the perfect gift for your new lady friend. To have a stunning view when she gets up every morning."

"Elijah. I feel like this conversation is one we have weekly. I'm really trying to not lose my temper right now. But, son..."

Elijah interjects before I can continue. "You haven't found the dead person in your room, have you? Well, half a person. It's Brad's torso, we found it."

A loud roar erupts from deep within. My lungs and vocal cords are giving it all they can when Thomas boldly speaks up, "Are you worried about bloodstains on the flooring? Because he was pretty empty when we finally got him."

Pinching the bridge of my nose, I say, "Do you do this in your bedroom with Rain? Or you, Thomas, would you do this to Greta?"

"Absolutely not. We have a room for that, and Thomas knows better than to piss off that old wench."

Then why mine? I don't speak it out loud; it's of no use. He won't understand how wildly inappropriate this is.

Throwing his head back, he cackles as if he just told himself a joke in his head. "She's nothing more than a whore. She's getting too comfortable here, don't you think?"

I don't budge, my eyes zeroing in on him, everything else is a blur. Am I having a stroke? Is this what finally takes me out? What the fuck is he going to do when he finds out I'm fucking obsessed with her?

I'm fucked. He's going to kill her.

"You can't touch her. She is technically our Queen," are the only words I am able to muster up while in the process of having my stroke run its course.

But he completely ignores me. "Do you know how Brad got there? Aren't you at all curious how we obtained him?"

Shaking my head, I reply, "Yeah, sure."

"Thomas, he is a loyal servant. And the rest of the bodies are from the cabin, Hell Fire Night, and the backwoods."

"Clean this shit up. My room is your priority," I snark while trying to figure out how the fuck Thomas got that close to Dalton's compound without becoming another body decorating my backyard.

Elijah answers for me. "His face, it's unmemorable, so he blends in. People who did see him thought he belonged there."

"Right then. I will leave you boys to it. Perhaps the pigs would appreciate some of the many treats from my yard, yes?" This is not how I expected to start my day, not with all the other shit going on around us. But Elijah doesn't realize that, reading the room is not in his wheelhouse.

Then it occurs to me.

Elijah is training Thomas, grooming him even, to be his own personal pet.

Fuck my life.

RYLEE

Nathaniel stormed out, only throwing his trousers and dress shirt on before leaving me here, alone, once more.

Rogers knocked on my door moments later, followed by two females rolling in multiple suitcases filled with my personal things from The Ranch. My first instinct was to call Greta, but as I reached for my phone, I questioned myself. Is it safe to contact her if I am being forced to hide out here?

I miss my life, my bed… my home.

I want to be grateful that so many people care and

love me. They are doing everything to protect me, but a part of me is still so fucking resentful.

All the families were destroyed because of The Exiled, including their own members. And they just continued to go along with it, until now. Why is it now such a big fucking deal?

Thoughts are frantic and my body still feels exhausted. Perhaps I'm overthinking everything.

Walking to the suitcase closest to me, I sit cross-legged and begin sorting through my things; it's a mix of comfy casual and latex. They are neatly folded, ready to be put away. Taking a stack of tees out, the back of my hand rubs against something smooth and familiar. Lifting the shirts out, I see my baby. My flogger. Metal staples stare back at me, and I smile, finding comfort in seeing it.

I place the tees next to me and reach for the handle. Standing up, I catch a glimpse of myself in the dresser mirror and decide, this time I want to watch. Sliding my shirt off, my body is exposed. My breasts are round and full, my hips are curvy, which I've always been proud of, and a backside that I've recently learned how to clap. But I've lost weight. I can see it in my face and legs, and I don't fucking like it. Just like I don't like how weak I get around Nathaniel Sinclair.

Turning my body, I grip the leather handle of my flogger. With my other hand, I slide my hair off my shoulder so I can see my back in its entirety.

Old wounds are healing, scabs are forming. It's time to reopen them. I must not give in to my own temptation and desires during sessions; he's made me throw my discipline out the window multiple times, and I fucking hate myself for allowing it.

The sharp staples poke through my skin with the first whip; the sting of the leather tassels follows. But it doesn't stop me from lashing myself again.

Get your head in the fucking game, Rylee, I tell myself as I crack my skin once more, this time opening an existing wound. A trickle of blood streams down my spine. It's beautiful.

I keep going, not letting up. It even starts to feel good—so fucking good. More blood stains me, my teeth bite my lip, and my nipples harden. Call it what you want, but I'm starting to love it.

The last time I put all my power behind it, bringing the flogger forward then rapidly swinging it back onto my skin.

"Fuck," I hiss. This one really hurt. The staples embed themselves into the shoulder blade. Lifting my hand, I pull at them, and my skin tries to lift and tear. I keep holding it this way for a couple minutes, applying more pressure once it starts to feel comfortable.

I don't deserve to enjoy this pain.

My hand opens, letting go of the flogger, and it dislodges, falling to the ground behind me. Looking in the mirror, I admire my handiwork, all deserved, the old and the new.

Red droplets that were slowly moving down have stopped and are beginning to dry. Satisfied, I reach for my shirt and slide it back over my body.

The curtains are open, the clouds break, and daylight peeks through. I try to ignore the dozen bodies in Nathaniel's yard, but it's nearly impossible. I've never seen anything like it. It's still shocking as my eyes examine each body or appendage for the millionth time.

Behind me, the bedroom door swings open, startling me. My heart nearly jumps out of my chest.

Turning toward the intruder, it's my silver fox, accompanied by an unforgiving odor. My nose turns up, and my face scowls.

"We are going to see your cousin, Cecilia. Be ready in twenty; I need to shower first."

I nod, taking him in. This man has a way of making me feel shy and uncomfortable.

"May I join?" The question barely makes it out of my mouth. I fear rejection and hate myself for asking. Impulses are taking over. It's clear I'm no longer rationally thinking. When I am with a client, no rejection, no vulnerability, but this is becoming more than just a transaction between Nathaniel and me. A wave of realization washes over me. Instinct tells me to keep fighting it, this man and what he had believed his entire life are fucking evil and he must pay. But the reality is, Nathaniel Sinclair is becoming my caretaker, keeping me safe, protected, and provided for. He doesn't limit me or force things. And I think I like it. To not have to be strong all the time is something I didn't know I needed.

Nathaniel's words resonate with me. *'It feels nice to not think, to just be and do.'*

Scratching his beard, his face contorts. "Maybe we should use yours? Elijah left a gift in my room." I laugh, that motherfucker really is a psychopath. I suppose it's a good thing he is on our side.

15

NATHANIEL

This seems all too familiar. Just the other day I was watching *her* in my shower, now I can feel her watching me. Lathering my body with soap, I'm on a mission to remove any lingering pig shit smell from my body. This, by default, is also removing her phantom touch from my skin. The one thing that remains is the feeling left behind from the plug, a mixture of fullness and being stretched out is the only way I know how to describe it.

A cool breeze chills my back, the sound of the shower door closing follows. Turning around, I let the water fall over me as I take in her beauty.

The shower has multiple heads, two on the ceiling and a couple on the wall. Rylee steps in next to me, soaking her body and washing the day away. Her hair is pinned up so as not to wet it, a strand has fallen out, and it takes everything in me not to tuck it behind her ear.

"Does Darian and Cecilia know we are coming?"

"Yes, I told D we would be there within the hour." Acknowledging me, Rylee nods her head. She looks tired, so much has been dumped on her these past days. I'm impressed she's still standing. Many would crack from the pressure, but not her, she's strong, taking it all in stride.

Following suit, soap is lathered all over her body. Spinning around, she makes sure it gets every inch. That's when the same marks capture my focus. Squinting, my brow furrows. Some of these are fresh, new and reopened.

"What the fuck is this?" I'm infuriated. My hand holds her shoulder and I spin her around, pushing her up against the cool shower tile wall.

She gasps, shocked by my reaction. My feisty girl wastes no time slapping my face in response. The crack of her hand against my skin echoes, and the water running down my skin adds another level of sting to it. She would be happy to know this, but I show no reaction.

Rylee is well within her rights of slapping me; I'm not acting rational, and frankly, I'm elated she didn't knee me in the balls.

I wear everything on my sleeve with her. Has she noticed? Did she suspect this reaction would occur once I saw the wounds, or did she forget about that before asking to join me in the shower? With anyone else, I wouldn't bat an eyelash, but her... she is different. Rylee is able to get past the stone wall I have up with others outside of the family.

But that shit doesn't matter right now; she is my priority, along with the lacerations decorating her back.

"Explain." There is no need to elaborate, Rylee knows exactly what I'm pissed off about. My face is in hers as I look down, only mere inches from her lips. Our noses touch and lashes tangle in one another's. Her breasts are pushed against my chest, our bodies connected while I box her in with one hand on either side of her.

Her eye contact remains steady, defiant, and her posture is strong.

"Help me understand, please."

The pressure of the tile is too much, blood is dripping down behind her, pooling at her feet mixed with the water. Still, Rylee is unfazed.

I try a different approach. Instead of speaking to her like someone I care about, I speak to her like a business associate.

Time to bargain.

"I won't ask you to stop. Hurt yourself until your heart is content, I don't fucking care. But help me understand why someone who demonstrates such strength and power in public and with clients needs to do whatever the fuck it is you do to your back." My teeth are clenched and nothing is kind about my tone. If she wants to be treated like shit, I will.

"You can't bullshit a bullshitter, Sinclair." She thinks she has me, which is laughable.

"I'm afraid you have forgotten. Yes, I am protecting you. With the current situation in our town, you need it. I have given you food, shelter, access to your family, and the ability to continue working on me. But I can take it all away. This is still an arrangement, Ms. Vandenberg. Once Dalton is handled, I will give you a stack of cash and send you on your way, just like the others." I know this stings, because it fucking killed me to say it. My face remains stone, uncaring, but hers flinches. She is hurt.

She swallows back the feelings generated by my venomous attack.

Rylee pushes my chest. "Fuck you." But I don't budge.

"Tell me and I will go away."

"I hate you."

Winking, I smirk. "Good."

A scream erupts from her; it bounces off the glass

surrounding the shower and violently attacks my eardrums. I have learnt she can also be a tad dramatic.

"For some fucking reason that I can't explain, my pussy likes you. I have lost control of her, and I never lose control. I always maintain discipline and restraint while in a session, but she," Rylee points to her bare cunt, "has decided to stop listening to me. It enrages me." Her tone is more serious as she continues. "I pride myself on my ability to be professional. The marks are from me punishing myself... lashings. I must do better; I will do better. Do you understand?" She winces, and I wonder if this is the first time she has said this out loud.

"If this were a casual hookup, it wouldn't matter. But like you said, this is still an arrangement, I am on the clock, and this is unacceptable on my part."

I hear what she's saying. To a degree, I even understand it, but I wish it wasn't the case.

"This is the first time since I first started my dungeon, professionally working within this lifestyle, that this has happened to me. At the start, it did once or twice, but I trained myself, my body to behave unless it was a part of the session. And how my pussy has responded to you is not included in that small percentage." It's fair, she is trying to hurt me like I did her. I am why she is hurt, bleeding into the shower water, and I hate it.

My ex-wife popped pills 'because of me' but I didn't give a fuck. But Rylee... She's different.

Our eye contact is still intact when the next sentence leaves my mouth before my brain can stop it. "We've never kissed," I state matter-of-factly.

Rylee shakes her head slightly, her response short. "And we won't."

"Understood." On the outside I appear unfazed. Internally, it fucking kills me to hear it. I know I'm the one who just laid into her because I am an asshole, but the need to understand outweighed being nice about it. Why does she have to be so fucking different?

We stand in silence, and warm water trickles down our bodies while neither of us move. Whether she admits it or not, this moment is intimate.

I've shown I care enough to then hurt her with words.

She has shared a vulnerable part of herself with me, then snapped back, putting me in my place.

Rubbing my lips together, she bites hers. They are so fucking sexy and full, I just want to bite into her bottom lip and suck it into my mouth. Her big eyes look at me, waiting for me to do something, anything. I can feel my cock getting hard. Shit. Flexing my toes, I try to redirect the rushing blood elsewhere to no avail.

"Hurry up, we need to get to the hospital."

Breaking off from the sexual tension, I step back, freeing her from my hold, and leave the shower. This isn't the last time that we will speak about this, and her self-discipline techniques, but for now I will let it rest.

I can hear her murmur, "Asshole," under her breath as I grab a plush white towel from the heated rack.

"Yes, you were just there last night, darling," I holler back, leaving her alone in the bathroom.

16

RYLEE

The elevator ride to Cecilia's private room is quiet, similar to the car journey here. Everything smells like death and sanitizer. As we were pulling out the compound, looking back in the side mirror, I saw Thomas and Elijah dragging something wrapped in plastic across the street. Rain was on the end of their driveway with her arms crossed. I would be shocked if she wasn't mumbling obscenities, and she's having a baby with Elijah. The woman is a saint.

The elevator stops, the steel doors slide open, and stark white walls greet us. Nathaniel, who is wearing a crisp white V-neck tee, jeans that hug his tight ass perfectly, black framed glasses, and black combat boots leads the way. Lifting his inked hand, he waves for me to follow him. "Puppet, this way." He's calling me that to piss me off. I am not his goddamn puppet, not after this afternoon.

I try to show restraint and focus on the space around us.

The halls are sparse, with minimal staff, and there are no signs of other patients whenever I glance into a passing room. Ahead I see two people standing guard. Pride fills my chest as I notice one is a female. Fucking badass. They are standing against the wall with a closed wooden door separating them. This must be Cecilia's room.

"Where is everyone?" slips from between my lips.

Nathaniel is quick to respond. "Secured floor."

The Exiled are connected, this shouldn't surprise me, but it does. This is a hospital where sick people should be getting tended to, yet they have managed to shut down an entire floor for a girl. Reason number seven thousand four hundred and thirteen on why I hate them. The level of entitlement is appalling.

"And before you get on your high horse, these two are Antichrist."

Rolling my eyes, I'm still disgusting.

But he doesn't stop there. "And D and I have accommodated the other patients in this wing at a neighboring town's private facility. We need to keep her close, familiar, and in our own territory."

What does he want—a round of applause or a Nobel Peace Prize for him and his little buddy?

Reaching the door, the two guards give Nathaniel and me a nod, allowing us entrance into the room. We don't knock, instead, we walk right in. Immediately the beeping of machines catches my attention, they surround one side of Cecilia. IV bags and cords lead to the frail girl asleep in the bed. Her eyes have dark bruising around them, cuts with stitching to help heal them, and a brace keeping her nose straight. Moving down her body, her blanket covers most of it, but her exposed arms and hands are just as bad.

What did they do to her?

A deep voice startles me. "They had her hung upside down, attached to a cross... naked. She was barely recognizable. They beat her..." Darian's voice cracks. He looks exhausted; this is a broken man. "I thought she died. I thought they raped her before killing her. I thought it all happened because of me. But then we found a pulse, a rape kit eliminated my second biggest fear, though some of it did happen because of me and who she is and what she meant to him. She was promised to him but I promised her to me, and she ended up liking it. But the biggest reason this all happened was because Dalton has a death wish, and I will happily fulfill it."

Nathaniel walks to stand next to his best friend, hand on his shoulder. "We will, brother. I promise. Things are in play, trust me." I wince, but I'm curious. Was Brad's head in his yard a part of this plan?

"Some of it has moved up the timeline, thanks to my boy. He did some redecorating today. But we will get that son of a bitch right where we want him, then make him pay."

Darian's head hangs, and he nods in understanding while clenching his fists.

Feminine grunts pull my attention. Cecilia's head is slowly moving side to side. Darian jumps forward, stroking her hair and whispering into her ear, "It's okay, baby. I'm here. It's just a dream."

Night terrors. She's going to need therapy after this; you can't survive all of this and keep it in. It will only kill her from the inside out.

Without hesitation, my body moves forward and my hands hold hers as I stand next to the bed, trying to comfort her. I'm a girl's girl and we stand and stick together.

The pad of my thumb rubs circles against Cecilia's hand, it's ice cold, likely from her injuries and lack of circulation.

Cecilia's lips move and her teeth begin to chatter. Darian's lips meet her forehead and hushed words are spoken, trying to coax her out of her nightmare.

It takes time, but her eyes start to flutter open and her body tenses. Right away she sees me and becomes breathless. "Who is she?" Cecilia says, panicked.

"No, baby. It's okay, she's with us. Rylee is here to

see you. She's your cousin," Darian explains before my presence sends his wife into a panic attack.

Hesitation follows, rightfully so. It takes a few moments for his words to resonate with her. "Okay," is finally whispered and relief washes over me. I never want to trigger anyone and it would have killed me if my presence did that to her.

"We are going to give you two some privacy. Darian and I will be right outside; no one is getting in here. I promise, Ceci. I would suggest your husband go home to shower because he stinks like sweaty boxers, but we know how that conversation will go," Nathaniel tries to joke to lighten the mood. His hand is still on Darian's shoulder, and he squeezes it. "Let's go, brother."

He nods, then makes sure this is okay with his wife. "Are you okay with that?"

She looks at the three of us, scanning the room. "I'm still so tired. But yes, just for a couple minutes."

"Thank you," I pipe up, still holding her frail hand. Cecilia's head turns to me and a half smile forms on her face. At the same time, Nathaniel takes the spare chair and brings it over to me so I can sit. I don't thank him, he needs to eat a bag of dicks before he hears those words from me.

Lowering to sit, I keep my focus on Cecilia but speak to the boys. "Go. Our five minutes of girl time has started."

Darian is hesitant, scared, and nervous to leave his

wife's side, but he fights his internal voices and leaves, following Nathaniel. I wait until I hear the door closing before speaking. "They may be old, but they still have impeccable hearing, it has to be the hearing aid implants," I joke. Her smile gets bigger. It doesn't quite meet her eyes, but it's getting there.

"My cousin?" Cecilia quietly asks.

Not only is family new to me, but also to her. We both lost our parents because of The Exiled. Yay, trauma bonding.

I don't dare say it out loud, I can be outspoken but I'm not a bitch on purpose... unless it's Nathaniel.

"Yeah, Greta just told me last night. I lost my mom to *them* too. I never knew the details, but always knew who was responsible." My gaze falls, and my breathing slows. "Brad is—was—my father. We found out Dalton killed him recently. He and my mom... Then I was born, which technically made me his heir. But he had her killed, silencing Greta out of fear, and later Brad had Dalton. Which is why the Antichrist started; she wanted to avenge her daughter and stop The Exiled. We aren't sure, but we think Dalton may know I am his sister, which threatens his throne. I'm staying at the Sinclair compound just in case," I finish explaining, giving her as little detail as I can, to not overwhelm her all at once.

Looking back up, her face is neutral, but her lips are chapped. Reaching into my sweatpants pocket, I pull out my lip balm and ask, "May I?" She nods, accepting my help. I squeeze the tube and apply some of the contents onto my finger before lightly applying it onto her lips. This moment is intimate, not sexually, but a connection is forming and trust is building between us.

It's my job to build trust, so it's easy for me to read once it's established and this small, kind gesture has done so.

Her warm breath tickles my finger as the cracked skin on her lips scratches against my skin. She still has an open cut that I delicately go around.

"You will make it out of this and be okay. And I promise to be with you through it the entire time, whenever and as often as you need me. We are family. We stick together." I've only ever had Greta; to have another family member is precious to me and I will not let this opportunity pass us by.

A single tear falls from her tired eyes, but I don't swipe it away. It's good that she feels and is allowing herself to.

Leaning back, her lips glisten and even with just that small change, she looks more alive.

"Cousins?" She whispers, still trying to grasp the concept I have had a head start on understanding.

"Cousins. I'm not sure how, but I am positive it involves some fucked-up family tree." I laugh thinking about it. "And technically, I'm the Queen of The Exiled. Fucking insane."

I notice her eyes move off of me and slowly shift to her hands. I follow her sight, wondering what she wants me to see. Cecilia rolls her hands over and I am shocked. It's mortifying. Bandages cover the area, but clearly that savage nailed stakes into her palms when hanging her on the cross. In one quick movement, my body rises and the chair is pushed backward.

"We are going to kill him, cousin. He will pay for his sins." I am enraged and unable to comprehend why this specifically prompts this powerful response out of everything I've seen or heard. But this is the last fucking straw for me.

Composing myself to not alarm or startle her, I relax my shoulders and look back at her softly. Her lip is quivering, and before I am able to apologize, she interjects, "Promise?"

The corner of my lip rises. This chick is a fucking badass. I am giddy with renewed excitement. "I'll record it so you can watch it over and fucking over."

"Thank you."

With that, the boys join us back in the room, always knowing when to ruin the moment.

Darian must see Cecilia's emotions riddled on her face because he rushes over, worried. Cupping her face gently, he looks helpless and defeated but also concerned. "What happened?" He is a man who is tired but is living and being strong for her, the love of his life. Cecilia is keeping him from breaking down; she is giving him strength, and I'm not sure Darian realizes that.

She lifts her hand and places it on his forearm. "Nothing. I'm just happy."

He is shocked by her response, and Nathaniel jumps in next. "We should leave them, Puppet."

My face must say it all because a tiny giggle comes from my new best friend.

For the first time since all this chaos has begun, I am excited for what the future holds.

I SNEEZE NOT ONCE or twice but three times; something fuzzy keeps brushing up against my nose and tickling it. My body is heavy from the most divine slumber I've had in years.

The tiniest little meow can be heard. My brow furrows, confused because I know Nathaniel Sinclair does not own any animals other than this deranged son.

Then it nudges my chin.

My eyes squint open, my vision blurry, and while I adjust, I see a black fluffy shadow. Blinking a few more times, everything starts to become clear. It's a kitten.

"What are you doing here, little baby?" I ask in

my cutesy voice, as one would do when speaking to the most precious thing you have ever seen. Light peeks through the curtains, allowing me to see it slightly better. The kitten steps back and paper crinkles under its paws. My hands pad around, trying to find the elusive piece of paper. Once I grab ahold of it, I sit up against the headboard and flick the bedside lamp on. My eyes adjust further, and I read the note.

Rylee... I'm sorry. She's yours.

- N

THIS SLY MOTHERFUCKER got me an apology kitten, and I absolutely adore her already. She won't solve anything, he needs to fucking grovel, but I will keep her and love her forever.

Placing the note down, I scoop up my new baby. Her collar is a beautiful rose gold chain link with a matching solid heart hanging down from her chest.

Proudly, I declare, "And I shall name you Karma."

Whilst I am basking in all this furry cuteness, a knock at my door interrupts us. Looking at my clock, it's just before noon, so it's not technically an inappropriate time of day to bother someone, but if it's Nathaniel, he can still fuck off. Words hurt.

"Come in," I shout.

The door cracks open, and to my surprise, it's Thomas peeking back at me.

"I initially came to grab you because I wanted to show you something cool I found, but now I see you have a kitten and nothing else matters." She is already melting hearts; such a good girl taking after her mama.

"Want to pet her? She smells like new kitten and I can't get enough." I am literally melting.

Thomas scurries in and reaches his hand out to pet her, but Karma hisses and he steps back with his hands up as if she is the police saying, *Stick 'em up.*

His words are rushed. "I come in peace," he pleads, but each time his hand comes out, she hisses.

"Has Thomas been up to no good?" I ask rhetorically and still in my baby voice.

Thomas is taken aback, but I know the company he keeps, so of course he has been naughty. But remembering his initial reason for coming to visit does pique my interest.

"Give me five and you can show me whatever it is you found."

He backs up toward the door slowly, keeping eye contact with Karma the entire time, not disconnecting until he is out the door and it is closed behind him.

With Karma scooped up, I get up and head to the

bathroom while giving her firm instructions. "Make sure you bite him if he's tricking Mommy. And always watch out for his leader with the skull face and the crazy eyes. Actually... all boys. Unless otherwise instructed."

I LEAVE KARMA INSIDE. I am already in love with her. The body farm is still decorating Nathaniel's backyard and Elijah doesn't appear to be in any rush to clean it up. Karma is still a baby; she doesn't need to be exposed to this fuckery yet.

In an oversized black sweater that hangs past my knees and a pair of soft Uggs, I follow Thomas to this mysterious thing he needed to show me out back.

It's a cold day and the crisp air tingles on my cheeks. I have my sweater hood up to help keep me warm. Following Thomas, we walk past the new decor, my nose turns up and my face screams disgusted. This is the strangest shit I have ever seen. Brad's skin is starting to sag off his face; his eyes are the worst, the skin isn't even attached to them anymore, and the hollows are visible underneath like the flesh there melted away.

Moving my focus, I look over to the white shed in the yard's far corner, all in an effort to keep whatever food is left in my stomach down.

Thomas points in the same direction. "This has some of the coolest stuff in it I have ever seen." I'm caught off guard. why is Thomas snooping around Sinclair's property?

My stomach drops, and alarm bells begin to go off in my head. "I don't think this is a good idea, Thomas," I say hesitantly.

Stopping in my tracks, I go to look around. Something feels off, and before I am able to take another step, hands fly over my mouth and a knife is raised to my neck.

"Keep walking."

Elijah.

Rolling my eyes, I humor him. He won't hurt me. Nathaniel would be pissed and Greta would kill him.

Thomas uses the special scanner to unlock the shed and opens the door, and Elijah pushes me in. The space is cold, dusty, and not well-maintained.

"Sit," Elijah demands, so I do by hopping up onto the exposed counter space.

Thomas closes the door and darkness welcomes us.

"I watched. I noticed, and I don't fucking like it." I can feel the venom dripping off each of his words; he hates me, and I fucking love it.

"Aw, you don't like me playing with Daddy?" I say sarcastically, completely unfazed by him.

An evil cackle erupts from his direction. "Play with

my daddy all you want, but get your leeching claws out of him."

Thomas clears his throat. "Boss, he has purchased her a kitten."

"Snitches get stitches, Thomas, surely Greta taught you that?" Karma was right, Thomas is a very naughty boy. I follow up, asking, "Where do your loyalties lie?"

"Ah, yes, Ms. Vandenberg. With the Antichrist and anyone who is a part of my efforts to remove Dalton from his throne." His words are shaky, he's nervous now.

Elijah slams his hand down next to me, and shouts, "This is my interrogation."

So, I invite him to continue, "As you wish, please proceed. But, Thomas, you should know, technically, I am your Queen; remember that the next time you are tempted to be disloyal to Greta and the family."

"You will never be recognized as Queen. The days of The Exiled are numbered. And if you insist on being called Queen, then I am forced to wonder, whose side are you loyal to?"

He's quick.

Turning my scare tactic against his servant against me.

Well fucking played.

"My cousin, Greta, and oddly fucking enough your family."

I can feel his breath on my face now, Elijah has

leaned forward. "Watch yourself, I don't always wait for permission to play."

Then it occurs to me. This is just a boy protecting his father. Not wanting to see him left hurt and heartbroken. He's noticed this arrangement is different from the others and is catching on possibly without realizing it and unable to properly articulate his feelings.

And, to be honest, I don't even know what this is.

"At least I got a kitten instead of pills." I take a low blow at his deceased mom, not wanting to let on to what I have just figured out. And Nathaniel isn't the one hurting me... because I am hurting myself.

Emotions rush up my face, I can feel my cheeks warm. Closing my eyes and holding my breath, I push them all the way back down. And I am grateful we are in the dark.

"I killed her. I hated her. He gave her pills to keep her tolerable. Then my step-father in his culty cloak and mask continued feeding mom's habit because he felt the same, found her intolerable. He only used her to get to me, his weapon." His words are soft and spoken against my skin, they send a shiver down my spine. At least he had a mother, but he doesn't have the capability to even understand how lucky he is.

I feel the cool tip of the knife against my throat once more. "I will kill you if you aren't careful. My dad doesn't always give me permission when I play."

His final threat packs a punch, because I know he

means it, Elijah has no reason to lie. We sit in silence, letting his words linger in the space around us, when the ringing of a cell phone interrupts it.

Thomas pulls it out of his pocket, and the light from it shines. Answering it, you can faintly hear a loud, panicked voice on the other end, but I can't quite make it out.

As fast as he answered, he hangs up.

His words are spoken fast, and his tone is alarmed. "We have to go. It was Greta. It's The Ranch!"

17

NATHANIEL

Fire reflects off my eyes. The flames are fifty feet away, but I can feel the warmth against my body. Embers are floating in the air, and if it were anyone else, I would think this was beautiful, but this is absolutely heinous.

This was a home. A safe space for people to conduct consensual business, but dickhead Dalton with his merry men destroyed it all.

Memories built here are all gone within minutes.

A loud explosion from inside The Ranch caused the roof to collapse and the exterior walls to fold in on top of itself. The fire department only arrived a few minutes before I did. There was no saving it, only containing it so the fire didn't spread to the forest surrounding the building or other rural homes in the area. Greta called me in a panic, breathless and almost speechless from being in disbelief to what she was witnessing. She was going to call Elijah next so I could focus on her granddaughter. I was at the house, in my office, and ran upstairs to grab Rylee, but only her new kitten was there, curled in a tiny ball on her bed sleeping.

There was no time to search for her, and there would be no reason for her to be at The Ranch, so I wasn't worried. Getting into D's Bugatti, I ripped out of the compound and headed straight to Greta, and now we are standing next to each other, witnessing the great destruction of her life's work and her family's home.

Shortly after arriving, Elijah sent a message saying he had Rylee and would be right over. I have no concept of how much time has passed since that correspondence was sent, everything seems to be moving in slow motion around me. Some of the girls and other employees stand alongside us in horror. Faintly I can hear their whimpers and gasps, but nothing seems real.

My phone goes off, which is still in my hand; my brain barely registers it, and my body doesn't move. When it goes off again, slowly I bring it to my vision. It's the two-minute later reminder. Time is moving, but I am standing still.

What I am reading doesn't register initially,

squinting with even my glasses on; I need to reread it several times.

UNKNOWN
You took my head, now I will take yours.

A HAND TOUCHES MY ARM, and I startle. Looking up, it's a distraught Greta. Her face is red and swollen, tears stream down her cheeks, and worry from the unknown fills her eyes. Stealing Brad's head was really fucking stupid. I haven't had an opportunity to further dive into that with my son, but it doesn't matter; it's done. It would not have stopped this from happening. But we can stop whatever they have planned next.

"They're here," Greta states while wiping her eyes with a tissue.

Looking over my shoulder, I see Elijah and Thomas getting out of the Range Rover, but no Rylee. Spinning around, I walk toward them. Elijah must sense my concern because he points to the back with his bat. "She's in there." I nod and rush over. He and Thomas pass me and go to Greta.

Opening the back door, Rylee's face is pale with wide eyes and a quivering bottom lip.

She's in shock.

I notice her hands are trembling in her lap and her leg begins to bounce in place.

From what sounds like a million miles away, I can hear Elijah shouting. More fire and rescue workers disperse around us, I think I see red and blue flashing lights peeking in through the windshield, chaos has ensued, but my focus is on her.

Rylee's beautiful, dark, long hair hangs over her shoulder, and a few pieces try to cover her face from me. My hand reaches forward and tucks them gently behind her ear. I then cup her face, my thumb rubbing her soft skin. "I'm going to fix this." It's a promise.

She doesn't acknowledge me; I am unsure if she even heard what I said, so I repeat myself. "I'm going to fix this, Puppet."

Her eyes shift to look at me. There she is.

"Where's Greta?"

Stepping back, I let go of her face and hold my hand out to her. Lifting her own, which is trembling, she places hers into mine and hops out of the back seat.

Moving her head slowly as she takes in the scene before falling into herself, loud sobs follow, as she covers her face with her hands. I move quickly, wrapping my arms around her in an effort to comfort. I don't speak, I just let us be in the moment, allowing us to both feel everything we need to.

This isn't just a house to her. The Ranch is the last

place she spent time with her mom, where memories were built and experiences were shared. This was Rylee's safe place and it's been stolen from her.

Neither of us moved; I could stand here for hours if she needed me to. But she breaks the silence with her soft voice. "How did he find out?"

I kiss the top of her head, my lips moving against her hair. "I don't think he knows." Blowing out a deep sigh, I squeeze my eyes as I continue. "I have reason to believe this has to do with the disappearance of Brad's head. It definitely escalated things before when we had originally anticipated everything to kick off. I am so sorry, Puppet."

Rylee sobs harder into my chest. Wearing just a white tee, I can feel her tears soaking through the fabric and my heart fucking hurts for my sweet girl.

Elijah always means well, but this time he has fucked up royally. And instead of him paying for it, Greta, Rylee, and all the others who relied on The Ranch are suffering.

Catching me off guard, Rylee's hands brace on my chest and push me away. My feet stumble over one another from the sudden movement.

"Get away from me!" she shrieks. "And stay away from my family."

I don't get the opportunity to respond because she is already walking past me to get to her grandmother. I love my kid, but today I am really questioning why. He acts so impulsively sometimes and never deals with the consequences of his actions, I am always left cleaning up after him. And I know he can't fucking help it, but dammit.

My phone buzzes again. Looking down at it, another message has come through, this time it's Rain, and whenever I see her or we talk, I thank whoever I need to for bringing her to us. And as I read what she's typed, all my reactionary resentment washes away.

RAIN

I gotchu, Papa. Our boy will have to learn one day lol.

SHE HAS SLOWLY STARTED to call me Papa shortly after finding out they were pregnant, maybe to prepare me, but a part of me hopes it's because she can trust me, and I protect and love her as if she were my own blood.

We are so similar, always on the same wavelength, and she can put Elijah in his place with the snap of her fingers, and it's a pleasure to watch. He can also bring out her crazy, which I always get a kick out of. They truly balance each other. Soulmates and partners for life, without a doubt in my mind.

But before Rain gets to him, I need him to do something for us.

Turning around, the house is pretty much gone; the flames still roar and everything is burning with the exception of the wooden swing set in the yard.

A few people come up to me. Their mouths are moving, but I can't hear anything they are saying. My mind is racing, planning and analyzing which move makes the most sense without risking more loss.

Dalton is reacting, he isn't thinking. He is likely celebrating this victory. Father like son, both arrogant and narcissistic.

I shout, "ELIJAH!" Everyone around me freezes.

Casually, he walks up to me. "Yeah?"

"Handle it," is all I have to say for him to understand.

He nods and calls out, "Thomas."

Right, because he can't go anywhere without his pet anymore.

Looking to Thomas, he says, "Involve the Antichrist."

He very seriously responds, "Of course, Duke."

They both take off to the waiting Range Rover and peel out of here in a hurry.

I give Greta and Rylee space to mourn and keep an eye on them from a distance.

Pulling my phone back out, I message D.

It's go time, brother.

HE RESPONDS WITH A THUMBS-UP.

FABULOUS. His enthusiasm is always top fucking tier.

Hair has fallen over my forehead, my fingers push it back, with Rogers being next on my list of people to call. He answers after the first ring, eagerly, but I speak before he can. "We need to find a house for the others to work out of that's safe. I don't want them losing money or clients because of this shit." I don't wait for his response before hanging up, simply because I don't have time to waste. I then send a quick message to Ryder, letting him know that shit is maybe going down. He is supportive and offers help if needed.

The parts are moving and the pieces are in play.

Things that would normally stress people out get my dick hard. This is my championship game, the final battle in the war, and we are going all fucking in.

18

NATHANIEL

We dropped Greta off at Rain's on the way home. I fucking love my daughter-in-law, but Elijah is going to lose his shit when he sees who is staying in his guest room for the immediate future.

"If she ends up dead because of your kid, I'll fucking kill you." Puppet's gaze is focused out the passenger-side window. I want to laugh but can't; her words are robotic and lifeless, like she isn't really here. Parking the car, I turn off the engine and sit with her in the silence of the space. Rylee's entire life burned and crumbled before her eyes, but by the time we left, it was gone, all of it.

She's lost her mom twice.

First the real version that would tuck her into bed at night, and then the memory of her. Reaching my hand off the warm leather gear shift, I touch her knee softly in an effort to comfort her but she doesn't want it. Rylee brings her legs into herself, turning her back toward me and she continues to look out the window.

My head rolls against the seat. Looking up at the car ceiling, I feel helpless. As much as I have been there for my son and supported him through his journey in finding himself, this is completely different. She is completely different. I can't make her feel better by giving her a hit or a new person to mutilate. I don't know what she needs, but it seems like I am not it.

Do I go get her cat? I don't know.

Restlessly, I start playing with my rings, twisting them relentlessly. The longer we sit, the more my sympathy turns into impatience and frustration. And this isn't the time to make any of this shit about me, but I can't resist. Slamming my hands on the steering wheel, "We don't have time for this," escapes my mouth before I am able to stop it.

Rylee turns slowly and I know I'm fucked.

Her eyes are red and puffy from crying, her face is in a scowl, and her fists are clenched. She is going to punch me, and I keep my face relaxed and ready because I deserve it. And honestly, we don't have time for this shit, but I shouldn't have said it out loud.

Her knuckles connect with my jaw, skin cracking against skin. My head jolts to the side from the force of her punch. I resist moving to rub the area once she pulls back, letting the sting sink in followed by the aching of my jaw. My eyes tear as a side effect of the hit, and I am able to sniff the nose drip before shit gets gross.

Unbuckling my seat belt, I jump out of the car and walk around the front. Passing the hood, I slam my hand down on it hard, convinced I could have very well dented it, but it's not even mine, so, oh well.

Swinging Rylee's door open, tears are welling in her eyes, dying to stream down her beautiful face, but I've had enough of them for the day.

"You can cry and scream and punch me after this is over, I promise. But I need your head with me right now. We destroy this motherfucker, then we cry. Can you do that for me, Puppet? Please?" I'm not beneath getting on my knees and begging, actually, I know she would love it. But it's my turn to have her back, to be the person she can lean on. So I reach over and unlatch her belt, then pick her up bridal style out of the car. She is slapping my chest, kicking her feet with tiny, cute grunts.

Walking to the front of the car, I toss her on the ground. She lands on her feet and places her hands on the hood to brace herself. Standing behind her, I growl, "Don't fucking move." Her breath hitches nervously as I undo my pants and free my aching cock, because, yes, her hitting me instantly got my dick hard.

I tug her pants down and push her oversized sweater up slightly, leaving her beautiful peach on display for me. A trail of spit drips off my lips, falling between the soft cheeks of her perky, fine ass.

"I got you, Puppet," is all I say before ramming into her wet, tight pussy. Her back arches, a loud moan follows, and her cunt immediately grips me. She loves my piercings and squeezes me harder in order to feel each one rubbing against her walls.

My hands grip her hips with all my strength. I want her to see me after, claiming and possessing. And a little pain feels so fucking good.

It's time to show her how I fuck.

"Touch yourself, Puppet," my voice rasps, instructing her, and she listens. Her hand rubs aggressively against her clit, edging herself further, taking her to where I fucking need her to be. Our skin slaps against one another's as I continue fucking her relentlessly. My cock is pulsating and our time outside could be short-lived, but I'm not embarrassed because she needs this as much as I do.

Panting, I tell her, no, I demand her, "Use me. Take it." She purrs as her leg begins to twitch and her breathing becomes heavier.

"Oh, fuck yes," she pants.

And don't you worry, sweet Puppet, I won't stop until we are both fucking satisfied.

Sweat beads on my forehead as my cock spasms inside of her. Every part of me wants to come inside of her, filling her with my release, but seeing my cum on her ass calls to me more right now. Pulling out, I let go of her hips and grab my swelled cock as ropes of cum shoot out, decorating her backside. My eyes are hooded as I take in the most beautiful sight. Rylee follows, her hand slows down, and she places her head against the cool metal as soft moans escape her. She places her hands on either side of her body as she rests, riding the waves with trembling hands. I begin to rub my release into her skin. "Don't clean it off," I instruct breathlessly.

Huffing, she promises, "I won't."

Reaching down, using two fingers, I scoop her cum onto my fingers and then rub my cock with it. A hiss leaves my lips as I tug my pierced cock, coating myself in her. It's possessive and she is claiming me without even realizing it.

Slapping her ass and ruining this moment completely, but someone has too, I say, "Pants up, Puppet. We have shit to handle."

Begrudgingly, she whispers at me, "I hate everything you stand for and who you belong to."

A shot to the heart, fuck. "I know. And I promise I am trying to make it right. I will fix this."

RYLEE

Hours have passed, the sun is setting, and my mind is still stuck on what happened this afternoon in the driveway. I've never been fucked like that. I have never let anyone fuck me like that.

It has always been me in control. Because I like to be, and I've always been scared to let it go. You hear stories of awful things and as a female, you immediately put your guard up, then you grow up with Greta and you just grow up being a badass. I almost think it's hereditary as a Vandenberg.

I relinquished control, and everything was okay. My mind is in shock, but my body is alive. Electricity was rapidly flowing through it the entire experience, and when he told me to play with myself while his cock and piercings were rubbing all the right places, I could have melted. And for those few minutes, I was free and for once, someone else was taking care of me.

I haven't showered, his cum still coats my backside, and I like it, feeling claimed and worthy of it. Don't get me wrong, I know my worth and I am extremely confident and body confident, but to have it validated by someone you may be growing an attachment to feels so fucking good.

As I go to cuddle a sleeping Karma, I can feel the large smile on my face. I bury my face in her soft and fluffy coat and take her in, there is truly nothing better than a new kitten smell. I can't describe it and do it justice, but when you smell it, you feel like you're home; it's infinite love and comfort.

I'm sure people get the same way with new babies,

but the thought of a new baby makes me scrunch up my face, ruining my moment of solace with Karma. I've never wanted to be a mom. Growing up, I never had dreams of it, not because I lost mine, but because I never longed or desired for them. Greta has never pressured me, and she wouldn't. My body, my choice. And it's always going to stay that way.

A faint knock at my bedroom door disturbs Karma and I. Her precious large green eyes open, beautiful against her black fur, followed by the most adorable yawn showing off all her sharp baby teeth. "Yes?" I answer, not looking away from my new fur baby. The door slowly opens, tiny creeks come from the hinges, and I don't recognize this person. Rogers and Nathaniel open the door swiftly, but this is gentle, feminine. Even Thomas was more abrasive when he tried to trap me earlier.

Turning my head, I see a familiar face with long black hair and a black leather choker—no, it's definitely a collar around her neck with rose gold intricate detailing and surrounding a single vile of crimson red blood.

Rain Sinclair.

She has the biggest smile on her face. Wearing leggings, sneakers, and a sweater that is showing off her ever-growing baby bump. I smile back at her; her energy is warm, and I instantly know I am going to like her. Plus, she has Greta staying with her as a kind gesture and a way of pissing off Elijah, her partner. The girl is top fucking tier, really.

"I just wanted to stop by quickly while Greta settles in. I have a present for you, a sort of welcome to the family gift." Her statement shocks me, because I'm not with *him*.

The smile fades from my face and my eyes look at her inquisitively.

Rain brings her hidden hand out from behind her back, and in it is something shiny. The sun from the back window shines directly on it, causing an instant glare. Karma eyes it on the wall behind us and begins growling and entering pounce mode.

Dammit, she is so freaking cute.

Moving my focus back to Rain, I continue to analyze what she is presenting to me. She takes several steps toward me so I can get a better look. My head tilts, it's absolutely stunning. Reaching my hands out, I pick up the object.

My fingerprints leave marks on the silver, I will have to clean them off to keep it looking pristine.

Flipping it over, I try to understand how this object works. It has four rings for my fingers to slide through and a separate piece for my thumb. The index finger has an additional ring to keep it secure and is the only finger that would be completely covered. Flipping it back over, I slide it on. The rings slide down seamlessly, fitting me like a glove—pun not intended. Silver covers my knuckles, including my thumb. The index has silver going all the way up, I am able to bend, and I can see it is made of three separate pieces, allowing for movement. On the top, the fingernail is a long, sharp, catlike claw.

Tears well in my eyes, today has been long and devastating. Then you have this person who I have barely met coming over and gifting me the most thoughtful gift. What did I do to deserve such kindness?

Swallowing my sorrow, along with all my other overwhelming feelings, I look back up to Rain, who is still glowing, and whisper, "Thank you."

"It will keep him on his toes. Make sure he sees you wearing it at least once." She chuckles before winking. And she may just be my new best friend.

"Have you seen the backyard?"

Rain shakes her head. "Yes, when I saw him and Thomas dragging a torso across the street, I had to come see what else they did. Safe to say officially, all that remains of Brad is his head. His body was dinner for our pigs that night."

"It's going to start smelling out there soon, every day the temperature gets warmer." I really don't want to have to smell all the body rot.

"If it isn't cleaned up by then, we can play his games too," she says with spunk before turning around to leave.

"I'm sorry about your house, but we will make it right. And you're not alone, you have all of us now." Rain looks back before closing the door, her face comforting, and I believe her.

Nathaniel catches the door. He reaches up and stops it from closing behind my new friend. His eyes then notice what I am wearing, and they widen, freezing him in place.

Mother like fur baby.

I keep my pride tucked away and only allow him to see stone. "You'll get her collar engraved; Karma needs her name on it," I tell him while holding my new accessory out, taking it in.

Nathaniel is quick to reply. "As you wish, Puppet. But what are you wearing?"

His tone has changed, he is nervous but also extremely serious.

Rain waits in intrigue.

"Something we will play with later, if you are a good boy." My own tone changes to sultry and seductive.

He hisses, "Fuck," under his breath.

Then it occurs to me, father like son, they both have a fascination with rose gold collars.

Peculiar.

Rain excuses herself. "Papa, I should go check on Greta." She smiles at him with her eyes full of love.

"Please call if you need anything," he insists, and she rubs his arm kindly.

"I will, promise." Then she leaves us alone.

"How are you doing?" And as soon as those words leave his mouth, I am in hysterics again. Removing the cat finger claw, I don't want to rust it with tears. I set it down on my bedside, then cuddle back up with Karma. My emotions are a roller coaster of a ride and I hate it. Crying is something I find to be uncomfortable but have been told that it's also very healthy. I beg to differ.

I feel the bed dip as Nathaniel sits down, his hand touches my leg and gently he squeezes. "We will rebuild it," he rasps, choking up. Seeing me like this is clearly impacting him, and a tiny part of me is glad. He deserves to hurt like I am, for all the years of pain he and his organization caused.

"But what about work until then? It could take a year to rebuild." The sobbing gets louder at the idea of not working for another year. What will I do?

His throat growls deeply. His answer to my question will determine my next move. I can hear him thinking. Come on, Sinclair, you are a smart man, you can do it.

"Elijah's old shed out back. It's yours for you to do as you please." I know how hard that must have been for him to say. But this just determined his future without even knowing it. Getting up on my knees, and scootching over to him, I place one leg on either side, then sit down on top of his lap. I can feel his hard cock pushing against his trousers. Moving my ass on purpose, I encourage him to continue to be aroused. Nathaniel's breathing becomes more heavy, but he doesn't move to touch me, he knows I am in control right now.

He's being vulnerable. Allowing me to do the things I love in his yard takes a strong, confident man to be comfortable with such things.

When he promised he was going to fix this after fucking me over the hood of the car, I believed him, and still do. And as much as I am pissed off, hurt, and broken from the events of these past weeks, he is really trying. I can feel it deep within my soul. Anytime he enters the room, it's a connection no one could break, even if they tried. He would never lie or mislead me, purposefully. It's not in him, not when it comes to me or his family. Seeing how broken he is because I am, I know he feels everything I do, too.

"I still hate you," I tease through my tears.

The corner of his lip rises, a glint of hope entering his eyes. "Good. As you should."

"I will use my new toy on you, while you're asleep, vulnerable and unsuspecting." I continue teasing him.

His words are hushed but true. "I would be honored to die by your hand, Puppet."

Taking my hands, I hold his jaw in my palms. My

thumbs rub along his soft, pouty bottom lip, and acting on impulse, I lean in and kiss him.

My chest warms and my eyes close. Thankfully, he moves and grips my hips. I need to feel him holding me, and it reassures me that what I am doing is right. I use the tip of my tongue to part his lips, and his tongue meets mine. It's soft, unrushed, and passionate kissing. My nails play with his beard and lightly scratch his skin, bringing forward goosebumps onto his skin and my own.

Before it gets too deep, I pull back. Our lips unlock and I already feel lost and left needing more. Our eyes lock once more as my heart races. Nathaniel gently squeezes my hips, reassuring me that he's got me, like I have him.

Everything is about to change.

19

ELIJAH

"Thomas!"

It takes only seconds for him to poke his head into the garage where I am gathering supplies for this evening's playtime. His obedience is remarkable. I will give that old wench credit, she did one thing right training him.

"Yes, boss." And he is eager, like a little puppy dog.

Keeping my focus on the wall before me, full of shiny toys ready to be used, "I have a gift for you, Thomas. A reward, really. Your reliability and trustworthiness has earned you this," I praise him, as per the baby books I have been reading suggest I do. Allegedly, when one is given positive reinforcement, it makes them feel good, and they continue the good behavior. I have also tried this on my pigs when they are eating the bodies I feed them, and their curly little tails wag each time. This is one book that can be trusted.

Reaching forward, my hand wraps around the wooden handle as I lift the blade out of the wall mount. I had Rogers sharpen and shine it this morning, completely unaware at the time that this ceremony would be happening so soon.

"It would appear that my dad is displeased. The Ranch being burnt down is being blamed on us when it was clearly Dalton. So now, we get to play, and Thomas, you get to play with me this time." Turning around, I hold out the machete and present it to him. Thomas's face is one of shock, and I swear to fuck if he cries, I will throw it at him instead. I don't care.

Stepping forward, his dress shoes click against the concrete flooring. The guy is always in a suit, and today he is wearing a black one with a white dress shirt underneath. I've told him he doesn't need to wear this shit, but here we are. Another day, another suit.

"Your first weapon is not to be taken lightly. My dad gave me mine." I nod my head toward my bat leaning against the wall. "And now I give you yours. It's a classic, just like you, the machete. Out of all the options, I believe this one will serve you best."

Thomas is still in complete disbelief. "If you cry or hug me, I will kill you with it," I warn.

Shaking off any sign of emotion, he reassures me, "I won't, don't worry, boss."

Placing the machete in his hands, he grips the handle and blows out a deep breath. His thumb runs along the sharp blade, cutting himself in the process because he is a dumbass. Hissing at the sting, Thomas brings his thumb to his mouth and sucks on the cut.

He still has so much to learn before the baby comes.

"We don't have time for you to bleed or feel, do you understand? We have bodies to carve up, and you are pissing me off the longer I have to wait here," I growl as I begin to lose my patience.

Bringing his thumb out of his mouth, he replies, "Yes, boss. I understand. I'm ready."

"You did a fine job collecting Brad and assisting me in setting up the body farm. Now, let's see what you do when they are still alive." Warmth fills my chest as I close my eyes, visualizing warm blood on my hands, dripping off my fingers. They are still alive as it rapidly pumps out of them, I watch as the life leaves their eyes, satisfied in knowing my face was the last one they saw.

My cock hardens, but I do nothing to hide or stop it.

"May we reunite the father-son duo," Thomas states confidently.

My eyes swiftly open, irritated.

"Greta is coming to stay with us," Rain cheerfully interrupts me further. My head whips around to look at her sticking her head out of the house.

"The fuck she is." Pleasure instantly turns to rage, and it wastes no time filling my body. The muscles in my hands twitch. I reach for my wooden bat with the intention to use it on the old hag.

Placing her tiny hands on her ever-growing belly, Rain's tone changes and she knows exactly what she's doing to me.

Fuck.

That tummy has me on my knees every night, eating Rain's pussy, and I fucking devour it. If I pull on her clit piercing with my tongue, it triggers a waterfall like nothing I had ever experienced before. So she knows, whenever she rubs her bump, I cannot resist and will do whatever she demands if it means I can feast on her later.

Greta will be our new roommate, but she never indicated if Greta had to stay alive during her stay. I grip my bat harder, my knuckles turning white, and it is taking every ounce of power I have to stop myself from playing with Denture Dolly.

Rain smirks in an effort to distract me further from my racing internal monologue. "Now go play," is all she says before disappearing back inside.

A loud roar erupts from deep within, and I slam my bat down against the stainless countertop. "Get in the car." My tone is toxic and would make that old cunt shit her pants if she were standing here.

Thomas scurries around the Range and jumps into the passenger seat with his new prized possession.

"Let's fucking play."

It's DARK, we have been in the tree line for hours, watching and waiting. I don't mind this part—the calm before the chaos. To sit in silence and just be, I like it. It's what comforts me.

Dalton and his team will suspect an immediate retaliation. We parked a couple miles away and walked through the woods to get to his property line, which isn't secure at all. The guy is power-hungry, a fucking joke. There is no way he would have remained King for long, even if this shit wasn't all going on. His acumen for organized crime is at a staggering zero.

We have been sitting here for a couple hours, the sun has long since set and the moon is covered by overcast.

The last visible light in the house went off forty-five minutes ago, if my time estimate is correct. I can't check my phone, it would be too much of a risk because they would see it shining, revealing our location.

Wearing all black, I blend perfectly in with the foliage surrounding us. Thomas still has a thing or two to learn, and in time he fucking better.

In preparation of go time, he removes his cuff links, rolls up his shirt sleeves, and reaches for his machete. He left his suit jacket in the Range, I told him he wasn't bringing that shit with us. The thought of him wrapping the jacket around his waist while we infiltrate the estate disgusts me. I am a serial killer, a weapon, and my pet has a cape. Not a fucking chance.

IT'S TIME.

The compound has remained at rest. Not a single person has done a security walk around the perimeter since we first arrived, so he suspects nothing will transpire this evening. He suspects we are plotting, planning revenge, when in fact we have had this planned for weeks. Him burning The Ranch down only escalated our timeline.

Gripping my bat, I rise. Thomas follows my lead, holding tightly on to his machete. We don't speak, it's silent communication from here on out. He is learning quickly, interpreting my body language is something he is becoming an expert in. Walking out of the tree line, I make no effort to hide myself; to be seen or not doesn't matter as the same result will occur. I am not leaving here without Dalton.

Our shoes crunch against the long grass and twigs, and my bat rests perfectly on my shoulder as my eyes keep watch on the windows facing us. Still no movement, no security sensors—nothing here is stopping us. My teeth play with my lip ring. Something isn't right. It shouldn't be this easy.

Instinct follows, and the same feeling washes over me.

Could he be hiding out, not even here?

No, his ego is far too inflated to hide. If he had people watching us, watching them, I would have felt it and we would have been surrounded by now as we walk through the open field.

"Boss," Thomas whispers

"Not now. I'm thinking," I snap back.

"It's too quiet." The kid doesn't listen, *not now* doesn't mean keep talking.

Doing my best to resist *the* urge, my knuckles crack from squeezing my bat. "I know. Now let me think."

An owl calls out overhead. Tilting my head, I watch it fly off Dalton's roof and toward the woods behind us. Even this fucker knows something is afoot.

We reach the side of the house unscathed. Instead of tiptoeing around the place, I decide to make a grand entrance, taking away any element of surprise they may have on us.

"Follow my lead and do not hesitate to use that thing if you have to," I snap at Thomas.

"Yes, boss."

I find being firm with him is the best approach; it gets him all amped up.

We are nearing the front, the driveway lit with the help of the garden lights, the porch area dim, but not intricate enough to have anyone hiding on it. I take one last look around before hopping over the low-lying shrubs and hibernating flowers. Still no sign of anyone.

Thomas follows as I proceed, walking up the steps to the front door. A single floorboard creaks and I freeze in place, waiting for what I could have just triggered. But no traps or flying knives jump out. The door is thick wood, similar to my dad's place, and as long as nothing is reinforcing it on the other side, we should be able to get in easily.

"Thomas, on three, we kick."

He comes to stand next to me, ready for my sign. "One... Two... Three."

On three, we both raise our feet and with all our force, kick in the door. A loud crack then a slam follows, and we nearly break it off the hinges before it crashes against the wall behind it.

Stepping in, it's dark and silence welcomes us. I find comfort in it.

From examining the blueprints prior, I know Dalton's room is upstairs and that the staircase welcomes us almost immediately upon entry. Walking to the right, I nod my head, inviting Thomas to follow. Using my bat,

I reach it out to feel what's in front of me, so I don't walk into anything. What I don't anticipate is tripping, which is what I do straight away. I can hear Thomas patting at the wall once he hears my "ouf" from falling.

Before I can tell him to stop, he has already done it. The lights are on and instead of a cool white marble floor below me, it's warm, wet, and bloodied.

Thomas begins to stutter, "B-boss…"

Looking over my shoulder once I rise, shock radiates from him. Confused, I look to see where his eyes are looking and follow his line of vision while I shift my body.

"Fuck me," is all I can get out.

The main entrance opens to the living space, the stairs, just as I remembered, are in fact on the right side. But before me is a level of carnage I thought I was only capable of. This is worse than any Hell Fire Night in recent memory.

KING is written over and over again on every inch of surrounding walls and windows. At minimum five bodies are hung upside down, similar to how we found Cecilia, with nails in their hands and feet, naked. Faces are blue from all the blood that rushed to their heads and some trickle from the wounds. A couple are beaten; their ribs are bruised, with handprints around their wrists. My feet move closer to one, and I lift one female's head. She has a similar build and features to

Cecilia, which I find most interesting, but I don't recognize her from The Exiled.

"Thomas, check them," I frantically demand.

I think these are civilians.

He lifts the head of an older lady, with hair like Greta's but with a less saggy body. "Are you thinking what I'm thinking?" he asks.

"Check them all," I respond, knowing we are both on the same page.

Another looks like Darian, my dad, and Rain. She is even pregnant like her. Nails are hammered around the perimeter of her stomach; I only notice because the light bounces off them.

Rage. Black fills my vision.

He knew I was coming.

He planned this. He baited me.

Or he is more sadistic than I am, didn't plan this, and did it for his own enjoyment in order to get his dick hard.

Seething, I growl, "Find him!"

My boots stomp across the floor back to the staircase, where I see what I tripped over. Another body; this one is slit at the neck and doesn't resemble anyone of importance. Maybe he was a commoner from The Exiled that Dalton recruited then decided to kill. Blood stains the steps leading upstairs. I follow them.

Midway up, I look behind me. Thomas is not there. Instead, he is frozen in place, shaking.

"Yes, it looks like Greta. Now get the fuck over here," I snarl.

Startled, his head nods and his mouth moves, but I have no idea what he is saying as he rushes over.

Reaching the top, I peek around the corner. Two tall and burly older men are guarding Dalton's door. This is going to be fun. Dim hallway lights give us sight for when I step out from around the corner and start swinging my bat with my wrist. A slight smirk adorns my face, and neither of them move. "Bravery will not reward you," I inform them.

Both raise their hands in surrender, declaring, "He's yours. We won't stop you." Traitors, how interesting. I was hoping for more of a fight.

"Betrayal won't be rewarded either." I smirk, showing off my sharp fangs, hungry for blood.

Stepping forward, I crack my bat against the face of one. Their head swings backward, and their body follows from the momentum of my hit. From the corner of my eye, I see the other trying to escape, but Thomas takes one swing, slicing him from skull to mouth. Loud screams erupt down the dark hall, and blood splatters across my face as I take another swing. This one lands the guy on the ground. I can hear Thomas still going behind me as, "Die, motherfucker!" is being shouted, and I burst into hysterical laughter while bashing in the skull of my guy.

This feels so fucking good. My eyes hood in ecstasy. This is my drug, killing will never not feel this good.

A couple more hits, and I start to feel the floor against my bat instead of a skull and brain; that's when I know he's dead. Spinning around, I see if Thomas needs help, my chest still heaving from the rush. And to my surprise, the kid is absolutely covered in blood; his bright white shirt that could be seen in the dark is barely noticeable now as crimson drips down his chest. Then I see not only is the guy's face sliced in half but so is his torso, which is carved into an X.

The sight fills me with pride. "Well done, Pet!" I praise, patting him on the back. And hopefully this teaches him that wearing a suit to playtime is a really stupid fucking idea.

Stepping away from Thomas, I open the closed door and step inside the room. A single bedroom lamp is turned on, illuminating the space, and confusion washes over me. Why didn't we see this light on from outside? Looking up to the windows, I now see why. Blackout electric shades cover each one. Stepping closer to the bed, I take in the barbaric and pathetic sight before us. Dalton and his shaggy brown hair fill the space. He is basically starfished on top of the blankets in only his underwear. Drool runs down his chin, and the rush raging through my body dwindles then completely dies once I see pill bottles on his bedside table.

"Thomas, what was in them?" I ask.

"Ambien, boss."

He didn't do this to himself. He wanted a fight, he has been begging for it since Hell Fire Night. No, his team drugged him.

Rats. Traitors. Disloyal servants.

They deserved to die. And any other I find that was once a part of his merry men will die too.

I grip Dalton's hair at the base and drag him off the bed and pull him behind me past his old friends and all the way down the stairs. His body thumps along each step, but nothing is going to wake him up at this point until the Ambien wears off and whatever else they may have slipped him. As we hit the last stair, a grunt follows. I shout back, "Shut up," as if he can hear me.

I drag him to the front door, dropping his head, and it bounces on the floor before settling in place. I wonder if he's even alive.

Bending down, I place two fingers on his neck in an effort to locate his pulse.

Nothing.

Not good.

I try his wrist instead, feeling around. I press as hard as I can until I find one. It's faint, but he is alive. Which is a relief. I would hate for him to miss his own death. I definitely need him awake for what I have planned.

Looking around the room once more, I walk to one of the many *KING's* written in blood and touch it.

Still wet.

These were done today and recently. I spot a couple holes in the wall and figure he must have been losing it. Obsessed with the idea of something he could never obtain. Obsessed with anyone who wasn't an ally or who he was promised. He was hoping we would find these and know what he had planned for us, one by one.

There is one more female. Long black hair hanging down, nipple covers, and a set of metal handcuffs hanging from her wrists. This has to be Rylee. He fucking knew who she was to him; why else would her lookalike be up here?

Calling my dad, he answers on the first ring. "We got him. But you need to see this, Dad. Innocents, blood... it's everywhere. Like he knew this would be his last chance or wanted to show us what to expect. Dad, that old lady from the bakery, who looks like Greta but less old..." I am not one to be shocked by anything gruesome and gory, but I wasn't expecting this when we entered his home. I wasn't expecting to see someone who resembled my little bat and our unborn child dead on his wall. He knew I was coming and that this would set me off. So, call how I feel disbelief from this idiot actually pulling off a mass slaughter.

One thing he didn't plan for was his own team turning against him.

I can hear my dad slam his hand down against his desk. "Dammit. Send pictures. I'll get Greta's team to start identifying and contacting families. We will pay for the funerals. And anything else they want. Get the cleanup crew over there ASAP. Contact the morgue, let them know we have bodies coming in. This shit ends today, Elijah." My dad has always had the empathy I lacked.

"Understood."

"You know what to do next, son. We will meet you there."

Hanging up, I take the photos and send the messages. I also advise the cleaning crew that the three not on the wall go to my house for my pigs.

Taking one more picture, I quickly send it to Dad, showing him how similar this is to the other two venues. Dalton used the blood as paint, KING dripping along the walls of his home and the upside-down human crucifix.

"Anyone who needs to remind people of their status this often doesn't really have a status at all," I tell Thomas, who is now looking green in the face.

"It was your first kill. It will sit with you for a day or two, then you will get over it. And if you can't get over it, pretend like you have, because I couldn't give a fuck," I advise casually, while walking back to the front door. I don't hear footsteps behind me, again. Loyal fucking servant, my ass. And if he's waiting for coddling, those dead bodies nailed to the wall are the closest he'll get to that.

Annoyed, I shout, "Let's go!" over my shoulder while looking down at Dalton. I've decided that I'll have to carve a reminder into his forehead just before he dies, so he never forgets what he is. The King of Failure.

20

NATHANIEL

Mortified and disgusted.

Those are the only two emotions or thoughts I can register at this moment while taking in the photos Elijah has sent through. He even sounded speechless on the phone, which is unusual for my son, because things don't affect him. But something in that room did, which is concerning.

I continue scrolling, and that's when I see it—the pregnant girl with dark hair. Fuck me. And next to her, another girl with black nipple covers and cuffs, suspecting that was his way of representing Rylee. The only body not completely exposed is the older lady; she is facing the wall but still upside down with nails embedded into her hands and feet. The bastard left the old lady with some dignity before watching her die slowly.

Once reviewed, I forward the photographs off to D, who is still at the hospital with Cecilia. They hope to release her in the coming days; she's been awake more and eating. His reply is quick to come in.

D

Today.

ME

I SEND a thumbs-up back to him, purely for my own enjoyment. It gives me some light on this dark day.

Sitting behind my desk in only my sweats, I lean back in my leather chair and finish my whiskey in a single shot. The sun is peeking over the mountaintops, trying to rise, and I already cannot wait for this day to be over. My office door opens. I don't even look up, thinking it's Rogers, but to my surprise, a cute meow catches my attention. I want to smile at her, but I can't bring myself to do it. Peering up, I find a beautiful raven-haired goddess staring back at me with sleepy eyes while cuddling her kitten.

"I heard something slam, bad news?" Rylee's voice is raspy and really fucking sexy first thing in the morning.

Placing my glass back down on my desk, I lean forward, bracing my arms before me and clasping my hands and resting my head on them as I blow out a deep sigh, "Elijah found more than just Dalton. And I don't want you to see what I have, but I also don't want to keep things from you either. It's graphic and incredibly disturbing." The room is silent following my statement, and I wait for her decision.

I must be so lost in my head that I don't hear her approaching because I feel her touch on my hand first.

"Show me."

Lifting my head up, I reach for my phone, click on the photos, then slide the device toward her. Rylee reaches up, her finger swipes the screen one after another, and I watch her face to try to gauge a reaction, but it remains stone, unreadable. She nods a couple times to herself, then slides the phone back to me. The photo she finished on was the Rain look-alike.

"It's like how we found Cecilia in the warehouse. He left them upside down to die. The last photo, she likely went quickly. The added pressure to the lungs and lack of oxygen to the brain would have caused her to hemorrhage rather quickly into the torture." I pause, allowing her to absorb it all before continuing. "The others likely took longer and were far more painful. And unless the families request autopsies, I won't be able to answer anything about the baby. I'm sorry."

Karma is cuddled close under Rylee's chin,

comforting her mama. "Do you think he knew about me being his half-sister?"

I lean back in my chair, looking up at the ceiling, truly at a loss for words. "I really don't know. He may have, or you were there by association to Greta and myself. When Elijah found Dalton, his own guys had given him up, left him drugged, and laid out on his bed to take."

"Well, let's go. Take me with you; you're obviously going to see him and 'fix' things, and I have questions before that happens."

Raising my brows, I'm pleasantly surprised that she wants to witness what's to come. "We will do more than talking. But I can give you a minute to ask what you need."

Tapping her nails against the desk impatiently, Rylee snarls, "Let's go then."

Clasping my hands together, I smile sadistically, "It's a good day to die, isn't it, Puppet?" Rylee winks. "That it is, Mr. Sinclair." My cock hardens as the R rolls off her tongue.

This girl owns me.

THE SUN HAS ESCAPED over the mountain peaks and is now shining brightly upon us. I called Rain before leaving; she and Greta were already on their way to

Elijah, and she had informed me that they had seen the disturbing photographs. Greta was adamant that more people were helping Dalton than we suspected, more so after D and I declared our loyalty to the Antichrist, turning our backs on our brothers and sisters in The Exiled. And I believe she is right, he couldn't have done this alone, the boy is as dumb as they come. A mutiny was planned to get rid of Brad, then they would move on to us. It is the only plausible explanation.

"How will we get the names of everyone who aided Dalton?" Rylee inquires from my passenger seat.

"We have been gathering information since Cecilia was taken. We have some data, but I fear the pool is bigger than we originally thought. Hopefully after this morning more will come out," I vaguely respond. This is a game of chess, Puppet. I can't reveal all my moves before they have been made. Tapping the wheel with my fingers, I can feel her watching me. "What are you up to, Nathaniel Sinclair?"

"What's that old saying... Oh yes, curiosity killed the cat. And we can't have that now, can we?" I volley back. And just as I get the last word out, she is already slapping my arm and snarling at me.

"You leave Karma out of this." Which makes me chuckle.

"I would never harm her." I act taken aback by her accusation, causing her to roll her eyes at me.

It's been years since I have felt this light. Everything with her is so easy—the banter, the sex, and the need to protect and give her anything she's ever wanted. One look and it's hers. That's all it takes. But I know it's more than things or stuff for her because she kissed me. That kiss was the most significant piece of affection I have had in all my years on this earth. It changed everything and gave me permission and validation that everything I have felt thus far with her was and is real. Even though she tried to fight it and still does, her walls are slowly coming down and I will prove to her every day that it's okay to let me in.

Pulling into town, the streets are empty as the major headline is already rocking folks to their core. Word is out about the bodies found at Dalton's, and we may have nudged the paper to put it on the front page. We may also be their source, exposing The Exiled further and turning the town against them.

I feel my phone vibrate in my pocket. Looking at the time, I know it's now online.

"Check your phone," I tell Rylee, giving her an easter egg to the information she so desperately craves.

Her thumb scrolls quickly, then stops.

"Local biker gang was framed for the execution of our beloved chief of police weeks ago. It has now been revealed via our source that it was in fact The Exiled who acted outside of their Hell Fire Night ritual. The organized crime group has since had a massive change at their table where many former leaders have been removed or killed. The new Exiled now go by a new slogan of, 'New World Order'," she reads slowly in disbelief, but I don't elaborate.

"Oh my God." A gasp leaves her as she continues to read the article. "...Bodies have been found at the new King's estate, thanks to an anonymous tip that called in. It is being described as multiple bodies hung and exposed and nailed to the wall in what appeared to be an upside-down crucifix. It is also reported that all dead were alive at the time of the crucifixion and ultimately died due to lack of oxygen to the brain, resulting in a brain hemorrhage.

Allegedly this is a message to anyone who stands against them, and perpetrators remain at large. Do not leave your homes; it is not safe for civilians while the offenders are roaming free. The Ranch fire is also believed to be linked to the new leadership within The Exiled. The group's stance on female empowerment and the strong dislike toward its owner, Greta Vandenberg, who advocates for equal rights, inclusivity, and feminists, is what fueled the arson." I see her head shaking from the corner of my eye. I know Greta being an activist is pretty far-fetched, but believable in the grand scheme of things.

"D knew once I sent those photographs what to do. We are the source. We are the ones alleging. We are killing The Exiled from the inside out. I always keep my promises," I divulge. "A crew went in and began to identify the bodies. We are working with the morgue and families of the deceased to cover funeral costs. And we may have planted a few items for the police to find to better support our stance."

Her mouth is agape in shock.

"Puppet, close your mouth, now is not the time to want to choke on my cock. We have a King to kill."

21

ELIJAH

Dad pulls up with Rylee. I am leaning against the church doors, whistling while waiting to welcome him. This day has been a long time coming. I never liked the vast majority of The Exiled; I understood I had to participate and initiate in it, but I had no use for the organization. I would kill with or without them, they just gave me more available options.

"Thomas, welcome our guests."

He still hasn't changed from our adventures this past evening. Rushing down the steps of the Lord's house, Thomas's hand reaches out, greeting Dad and *her*. My eyes sliver, glaring at her.

I don't like her.

Dad takes Thomas's hand and gives him a firm shake before looking my way, and when he does, I give a little wave.

"Son, what do we have here?" he asks, rubbing the palms of his hands together. I can tell by how he's dressed that this is official business. A three-piece navy suit, his gold rings and cuff links, with a pair of dark brown curb-stomping boots.

"Your beard needs a trim, old man." He smirks then flashes me the bird before pushing his hair back off his forehead.

Muffled screams follow. Looking over, I see our friend has awoken again. The drugs started wearing off a couple hours ago, so I have been hitting him over the head with my bat to knock him out again periodically. I stuffed his mouth with some old rags so he wouldn't bite his tongue and bleed before I gave him permission to do so. And I find him utterly annoying, so it also helps with muffling his voice.

Once we got to the church, I dragged him up the stairs and tied him at his ankles and wrists, like a pig ready to be roasted, and we have been here since, waiting for permission to proceed. Dad wanted to be here for it, and apparently, his friend needed to be here too. If Greta shows up next, I am fucking out of here.

Walking behind Dalton, I kick him in the kidneys and tell him to, "Shut the fuck up." He groans in agony. Pussy.

"Take his muzzle off, son," my dad requests. I look behind him to Thomas, and he rushes forward, pulling out the rag, and tucks it in his pants pocket.

"Good boy, no evidence." Thomas smiles with pride from my praise, but then I glance down to his hands and notice something is missing. "What did I say? Where is it?" I snap, and he startles as he looks around frantically.

Racing forward, he snatches his missing machete. "I'm sorry, boss."

"Never leave it lying around. If this dumb fuck got free, he would have used it against you. It's the fundamentals, Thomas!" I spit, and he bows his head in shame, as he should.

"Elijah, focus." My dad pulls my attention back to him. Rylee is now standing next to him, and his brows raise questioningly, "And the others?"

Lifting my arms up like I am a preacher, I bellow, "Look up, look all around you. The heavens are singing to us. It's raining bodies." And instead of following my instructions, he laughs and places his palm on my forehead.

"Why are you touching me?"

Still chuckling, he replies, "Do you have a fever?"

I roll my eyes and give him a short response to his ridiculous question. "Look. Up." And I point with my bat to the tall stone arch of the church. His eyes light up; there hangs three Dukes, one Duchess, one Prince, and Chief Fredricks. Greta's people searched Dalton's for any clues while tidying the place up, and they found a notebook with names and payment amounts.

After snatching the book, they started rounding people up. This is all we were able to get in such short notice.

A thick rope was tied around their delicate necks and secured to the other end of the roof before pushing them off the ledge. A couple necks broke quickly. Others' deaths were prolonged; their feet dangled for minutes until they were deprived of oxygen and died. All have their hands restrained behind their backs, and the sight should be a photograph on my wall.

I point out, while he continues analyzing who we got, "You said no blood, so this is no blood."

"Jesus fucking Christ."

Confused, I look at him. "Dad, are we into that now? You know, Jesus?" Considering our location, it feels to me like it's a valid question.

Dad pinches the bridge of his nose, pushing his glasses up slightly, and squeezes his eyes shut like he has a headache. "I can't have this conversation right now, son. I just... no."

"It would make sense why you picked this place."

Rylee laughs behind us, and it takes every part of me not to bark at her to shut up. This is none of her business.

"No, Elijah, we do not do Jesus now. But you have done well here today. And for that, you will be rewarded. Bring the blood."

Before I can dive in, Dalton has some final words for us. "You must show people. Teach them where they belong in the grand scheme of things. The town should have been bowing down to us. Fearing The Exiled. But you let them walk all over us. You fucking old-timers were nothing but cowards. Pathetic. A thing of the past. I am our future."

"Good for you," I murmur to myself while taking the rope, keeping Dalton restrained.

I pull him up from his side, to his knees, and on the step of the church, and like the little bitch that he is, he shouts, "You can't kill me. I'll never die." Okay, champ, someone is delusional.

"You are crazy. Do you not see your friends above us?" He ignores me, so I move my focus over to my pet. "Thomas, cut down the spine, and don't you even think about stopping before then," I command. The only way to get over the first kill is to keep killing.

The tip of the machete tucks under Dalton's chin. I lean forward and whisper in his ear, "I hear if you make it through this, without a single word or scream, the gates of Valhalla will open to you, but I don't think Odin likes misogynistic assholes either. I also heard something about a million virgins waiting for you on the other side, but who fucking knows."

Nodding, I signal for Thomas to take my spot behind our soon-to-be departed. My leg is pressed tightly against Dalton's chest to ensure he stays upright while Thomas starts to cut. Pushing the blade into Dalton's skin, I hear the first slice, and my mouth waters. Using the weight of his body, he applies every bit of force he can behind the one continuous cut. Dalton screams, but I barely register it. Suppose he didn't want a million virgins after all, oh well.

I continue watching over Dalton's shoulder. Blood drips down the blade so beautifully onto the stone step. Each drip sends my body into a frenzy, wanting to make him bleed myself. But I show restraint, letting Thomas have his moment. His face begins to redden, and those puppy dog eyes bug out of his face while his mouth hangs open, yelling, giving him the momentum that he needs to continue on.

Cutting through someone's torso isn't easy. You have bones, organs, and muscle to work through, but once you get to the end, the results are so fucking satisfying. We are almost at the kidneys when I notice Thomas's arms are shaking, but he doesn't stop because he doesn't want to disappoint me. Skin continues to tear and separate, exposing Dalton's spine, and my fingers itch even more.

As Thomas reaches the end, his breathing is heavy as he looks up to me for approval. He yearns for it, and it's not something I give out easily. Looking down at his work, I nod. He's done well.

Stepping around Dalton's side, I glance at my pet, "Hold him up." Thomas is still shaking, holding his machete with one hand, but he takes the rope in the other so I can finish our friend off. Rubbing my hands together, I'm excited. This is something I've always wanted to try but never had the prime opportunity to do. The blood eagle.

"Hold him tight," I snark. My pet nods rapidly, pulling a slowly-dying Dalton into him.

Casually, I advise adding more salt to the wound. "The blood of your men, the same ones who betrayed you, lines his shirt. I promise, you can and will die. And the rest of your crew, we will get to them one by one, snatch them out of their warm beds, the safety of their homes, then slit their throats." A loud roar of laughter follows. I fucking love my life. Then I add,, "Oh, and she," I pull his head up by his hair, so he can see to whom I am referring too, "is your half-sister, and by blood right, our Queen." Dropping Dalton's head back down, he makes no effort to keep it up or even speak. The clock is ticking on his life.

Gripping his ribs, one by one, I pull them back from his spine and out with skin and tissue still attached. Loud cracks can be heard as I break each bone. I need these fuckers to look like wings. At one point I find myself standing on his legs to keep his lower body stable as I yank and arrange him. Once satisfied with both wings protruding off his back, I find his lungs next. They were once filled with air, but now they barely expand.

Taking them tightly in my hand, I squeeze hard, then toss each over his shoulders. Dalton's body trembles; shock is kicking in along with the lack of blood and oxygen. Looking down, my boots are lathered in crimson.

I can't wait to fuck my little bat after this.

Lastly, I swipe the machete from Thomas and slice the rope that's keeping Dalton's hands secure. As they drop to his sides, I allow the machete to do the same. Reaching down, I lift one arm up and rotate it until I hear another crack. I then jam it into his socket, followed by breaking his wrist with one quick flick. I do the same to the other side before stepping in front of him to get a view of my final masterpiece.

Rubbing the back of my hand against my forehead, I can feel the warm blood against my skin. I push my fingers through my hair, it's euphoric. The blood of my enemy is coating my body.

Thomas is still bracing Dalton, who I suspect is well past his expiration now. With his arms raised and his ribs and skin underneath, it does look like fucking wings. The internet was not lying. I'm not sure of the significance of the lungs being thrown over his shoulders, but it looks fucking cool.

"Just call me Picasso," I whisper to myself before

hearing Dad laughing behind me. Looking up to the church peaks, I shout, "Preacher, lower the rope!"

Dad steps next to me. "What else do you have planned?"

Crossing my arms over my chest, with blood coating my skin, I don't respond. He can see when everyone else does.

The rope slowly slides down. It is securely tied around the chimney, waiting for the cargo to be loaded.

Smirking, I say, "Yes, you heard that right. Not only did I claim this church, but the priest has a gun to his head and will do what I say unless he wants to join the party." Dad pats me on the back, proud and impressed. I can tell because he isn't giving me shit.

Thomas reaches up and takes the rope, tying it tightly around Dalton's throat. After knotting it a few times, he yanks on it twice, signaling the good preacher to hoist our mascot. It's slow moving but oh-so satisfying. Blood continues to pool, dripping down Dalton's back. Seriously, the coolest shit I've ever seen. He looks more like an angel than an eagle, and I decide it's even more fitting this way.

The preacher ties the rope off, then Dalton is raised slightly higher than the others as his body sways with his ankles still tied. Thomas joins me in taking in the sight.

I can't wait for the town to see our hard work.

Fucking beautiful.

NATHANIEL

The pride I feel from my son's actions is contagious. This has to be his finest work yet, truly.

Behind me, I hear a flick of a match being lit, and turning my body, I see it's Rain. She is standing at one of the metal garbage bins on the sidewalk, starting a fire. Under her arm I see black and gold masks with the familiar dead rose dripping blood logo. I nod at her in approval before she throws them into the dancing red and orange flames.

Taking my white silk pocket square out, I wrap it tightly around my fingers and kneel onto the church step. Carefully, I draw a large circle in the river of blood around us, followed by an upside-down triangle. Lastly, I find the center of the star and make one line down, then another across. In honor of those lost recently and years ago, for Greta and her organization, the Antichrist.

My eyes absorb what I have just done. There is no going back now.

Rising to my feet, I am met by familiar faces. D and Cecilia are on one side of me. Rylee, Greta, Rain, and Elijah on the other.

I do not take this responsibility lightly.

"We fucking did it." D grips my shoulder. My heart

is racing, and adrenaline courses through my veins as it all starts to hit me. We fucking pulled this off. Emotion fills my eyes, but I blink quickly to clear any evidence. Nodding my head, I allow myself this one moment to bask in the glory of our win.

Because we are now *The Devil's Society.*

HIERARCHY

Diablo(s)
NATHANIEL / RYLEE

Antichrist(s)
DARIAN / CECILIA

Demons
ELIJAH   GRETA

RAIN

Hellhounds
THOMAS   ROGERS

The Damned
NEW INITIATES BLOOD OR CIVILIAN

RYLEE

EPILOGUE ONE

Months Later

Spinning on his tiptoes with his wrists chained to the ceiling, I watch Nathaniel hanging naked and vulnerable with a black blindfold on, all from the dark corner of my dungeon. Looking around the dimly lit space, with red walls and black accessories lining the small room, it has everything from toys to tables, mirrors to my beautiful saltire cross and my beautiful black leather chair that I am sitting in now.

My legs are crossed, my black latex-covered foot swings as I take in everything around me. Pride fills my chest.

I pull on my high pony to stop any tears from welling in my eyes. Because I recognize how lucky I am to be me, free to express myself in ways that are true to my being. Many are not and it kills me inside.

Fuck. I shake my head of all outside thoughts, focusing back on the fine specimen before me.

Nathaniel kept his word and hired a construction crew the week following the events in the church. And I, out of respect to my very new relationship, only see three of my long-term clients a couple times a month, and I am never intimate with them myself, I only assist in feeding their needs and cravings. To be clear, Nathaniel never petitioned me to do this, it's something I wanted, to set the boundary in order to see where this went or is going.

Gingerly I rise while watching myself in the mirror, with black lace panties to match my black latex knee-high boots and black latex bra that has tiny gold chain's dripping over my midriff.

Next to me, I take the ball gag off the wall and slowly walk toward my prey, allowing the suspense to build. Reaching out, I admire my silver claw glove Rain gave me. I like wearing it during our sessions occasionally.

Nathaniel's been hanging for ten minutes already, waiting in anticipation with a hard cock and precum glistening. Standing behind him, I hush in his ear to soothe him while placing the ball in his mouth. My breath tickles him because I can feel tiny goosebumps rising on his skin, followed by the sound of his teeth clamping around the ball as I buckle it at the back of his head.

Using the sharp claw, I start dragging it down from the base of his skull, down his spine, applying more pressure the farther down I go. He shivers and moans, completely giving in to me.

"My good fucking boy. Aren't you?" He nods eagerly to please. I take my other hand and rake my fingers through his thick white hair then grip it at the base, pulling his head back toward me.

"Are you going to let me play with you? Do anything I fucking want to you?" I toy.

He tries to nod, but groans instead, letting me know he's ready. Before we started, I made him repeat our safe word to me. Devil. And if he can't speak, he knows to moan three times in quick succession and I will stop.

My nail reaches his bottom, his cheeks clench and his body rolls as I tickle that sensitive spot. Smirking with my black-painted lips, I step back with my heels clicking on the hard cement floor. Walking to the wall, I unhook my black paddle with silver spikes and brush my fingers overtop of it. At the same time, a fun idea comes to mind. Reaching up, I also take our bejeweled plug off the shelf. I only use this on him, it's special to us.

Stepping forward, I spit on the silver plug and waste no time inserting it into his rectum. Who would have suspected, Nathaniel is a man who loves ass play. He cannot get enough of it now that he's had it once. Once the plug is secure, I swiftly swing the paddle in one fluid motion and spank my good boy.

"Count with me," I hiss, and he obeys. Muffled numbers are shouted with each one. The wood cracks against his skin as the metal spikes add another layer of pleasure, heightening this experience for him. I continue to watch his cheeks clench around the plug. The tighter he grips it, the more it rubs against his sensitive taint.

We get to, "Four." Crack. "Five." Crack. Before switching cheeks and doing the same amount on the other side.

I see his body trembling. "You will not come until I say you are allowed," I hiss at him, holding the paddle just barely above his skin. "I will stop if you do," I threaten.

His body rotates in protest, soft hisses escaping him as the chains nip at his skin.

Yanking at his hair, I praise, "Good. Now stay still, we aren't done."

"Yes, Ms. Vandenberg," is mumbled through the gag, which pleases me.

I finish the other side and drop the paddle to the floor, the loud smack making him jump. I've taken his sight therefore the other senses are working overtime.

Next I take a single piece of red rope, and spin him

so he is hanging in front of me. His cock throbs, I take my gloved hand and move the sharp nail from base to tip. His stomach muscles flex; I take the rope and begin tying it around him, doing figure eights around and over the piercings before wrapping it tightly at his base and knotting it. Circulation is being cut off, and his cock turns beautiful shades of blue and purple. Nathaniel's body wiggles, the sensation is overwhelming, the buildup grows and the need for release increases.

Whimpers follow, muffled pleads and begging. "Please, please, Ms. Vandenberg."

Silly boy. Not yet, I'm still having fun.

Gripping his jaw, I squeeze, pinching his skin with my fingers. "The greatest gift is you at my mercy, begging at my feet and worshipping the ground I walk on. Now, shut up and let me play," I snap, teasing.

Fuck, I can feel my pussy dripping down my leg. And I am still learning that with him, it's okay to feel such desire.

Taking my mind off it, I lean forward and place his hard nipple between my teeth, teasing and pinching, as my tongue laps it. Nathaniel's body continues to quiver, I love edging him to the brink. Biting once more, I then pull back and trace his endless ink with my eyes, admiring his beauty.

Looking down, I see his toes flexing, and reaching behind I rotate the plug inside of him, and continue to watch his body language. Cries of need follow, I have him right where I want him. Chuckling to myself, I stop and grip the ribbed dildo next. Squirting lube on it, I pull out the plug, replacing it with the dildo. Slowly I inch it inside of him. Nathaniel's breathing becomes heavier and I can hear his heart racing. I get it halfway in before pulling it out. He moans in agony from the lost connection. I do this a few more times, teasing, edging, while each getting louder and louder reactions.

Edging the tip back in, I slowly insert it inside of him, working his taint by grinding it back and forth. His body reacts, riding the dildo in return and chasing his building release.

His legs tremble, his orgasm is building, and his head moves from side to side. But he knows better than to come without permission; the last time he disobeyed, I edged him three times a day for a week.

Looking down, I see distinct red marks coloring his skin where the spikes spanked him, and I smile in satisfaction knowing that it's my mark he wears.

More teeth chattering can be heard on top of the intense panting. The room is getting warmer and my own skin is beginning to become moist.

I move the cock faster inside of him, building and edging his release.

Wrapping one of my legs around his, I push the sharp heel of my boot into calf muscle then whisper,

"Come," while reaching for his swollen aching cock. I undo my tie and the rope releases the building pressure. Ribbons of cum shoot out of his tip, and a loud roar erupts from deep within his chest. White lines from the tie adorn his skin, around his swollen cock.

Nathaniel continues to ride the rubber cock in his ass, as his body trembles violently. I keep my leg wrapped around his and I can feel his muscles convulsing under me. His hips buck with each shot of release falling to the ground. My thumb tickles his tip as I gather his release and bring some to his lips. I trace along them, leaving a trail of himself on me, for him to taste once his mouth is freed. As his body calms, I take the dildo out and toss it to the chair. Undoing the blindfold and gag, I drop them to the ground.

My eyes watch with need, as Nathaniel licks his lips, he moans in satisfaction while he enjoys the taste of himself.

"You did so good, baby," I praise, and he smiles with heavy-lidded eyes.

I release my leg from his. Bending down in front of him, and I grab ahold of his cock, bringing the tip to my lips and kiss him. We never break eye contact. "Would you like to take a bath?" I ask in a soothing tone, and his head nods in response.

I lick his cum off my lips, savoring every drop, and rise to unlatch his hands from the chains. His arms immediately fall limp on top of my shoulders, which is to be expected as most of the blood is likely drained from them hanging up for so long.

Holding him close, he puts most of his weight on me as he recovers, and I whisper words of praise and gratitude into his ear. Aftercare is the most important part.

I tickle the back of his neck with my nails, and softly whisper, "Let's go, baby, we'll take a warm bath with salts then sleep. How does that sound? And maybe later, I'll let you drive the Aston, as a treat."

His deep voice graces my ears, panting, "Perfect, Puppet,"

NATHANIEL
EPILOGUE TWO

Bright pink, yellow, and blue party balloons decorate Elijah's backyard. Even the pig pen has streamers hanging off it. Because today is a big day for the Sinclair family, it is my first grandbaby's birthday.

I hear the back door close. Looking over, I spot Elijah holding the birthday girl. He is absolutely enamored and obsessed with his daughter, Sid Sinclair. Behind him Rain follows, her stomach poking out from under her tee. She is nearly six months pregnant with their second child. Never did I think this future would be mine.

Elijah and his tendencies didn't leave much room for companionship, but when he found Rain, his entire life held a new meaning. He started to show more fire and passion, and a willingness to learn and understand her human nature. He thrives on making her happy, how she felt becoming the most important thing to him. And now that's been extended to his daughter.

He still couldn't give two shits about anyone in such depth, and I am convinced he is still trying to kill Rylee, but it's fine. I've explained to her that if he wasn't fazed by her, that's when she should worry. Because she would have been dead already.

The Devil's Society was a rather smooth transition, considering the circumstances. We kept a lot of outside contacts, dealers, suppliers, law enforcement, banks, and academics, and many later even admitted they prefer dealing with us. We are fair, but firm.

Initiation nights are not announced and they are nothing like Hell Fire Night. We keep to ourselves and don't involve the town. Everything is internal; those involved in the lifestyle only. And no more masks. People know where they stand, they know the rules and that you either follow them or end up six feet under. We also had to take the bodies down from the church after a few days, as they started rotting with bodily fluids oozing out of their orifices. It was fucking vile.

Elijah was annoyed, but I told him next time we needed to set an example, and he could remake his version of the 'last supper.' And that poor priest, E is up his ass all the time whenever he sees the old guy. He holds his arms out and preaches about him being our new bitch.

To be clear, the priest isn't our bitch, but we do use the church, often for meetings, and other extracurricular activities. And the town seems to appreciate the new changes. Of course they were rattled by the events leading up to our takeover, but we've embedded ourselves within the community to help better it; while also fulfilling our own agendas.

I hear Rylee squeal first, rushing over to her cousin Cecilia, who just arrived with my brother, D.

I am one lucky son of a bitch.

D looks at the girls, confused, then heads over to sit with me, looking stressed. Shaking his head in disbelief, my brother whispers, "She's pregnant."

"Who?" I question back.

"Cecilia. We just found out before coming over."

I smile. Standing, he meets me as I embrace him, and joke, "You are so fucked, brother. They both will have you wrapped around their fingers."

"Don't I know it. But fuck." He pauses. I can hear his thoughts racing. "What if I'm too old for this?"

Stepping back, I laugh. "You are, but it doesn't change anything. You will still love that kid unconditionally regardless. I mean, look, I'm about to have another grandkid and couldn't be happier."

Then a loud scream startles us from behind.

Cecilia must have just told Rylee, she's jumping with glee. This catches the entire party's attention, and D takes the heat off his lady by announcing, "I knocked her up." Everyone starts to laugh then cheer. Congratulations roll in and I step back, allowing him to mingle. He hates mingling so this brings even more joy to my day.

Before I can make my way to my granddaughter, Greta barks at me impatiently, "Now where's that psychotic son of yours?" Yes, *she* is still living here.

The Ranch was rebuilt months ago but she's never moved in. Most of the girls returned and even a few guys. It's great, but Greta never returned. She helps run it, but has really passed the reins over to Rylee for the more day-to-day operations. It's a big step and secretly, I'm proud of her, because Rylee is fucking killing it as the house mother.

Pointing behind me, I reply, "He went to feed the pigs."

The cleanup crew from last night dropped off a few bodies to Elijah. He hates overfeeding them so he rations the bodies and feeds the pigs every couple hours. It's impressive, he cares for those pigs more than I thought he would.

And the body farm is still in my fucking backyard. And the worst part, we are used to it now. The smell doesn't bother us and sometimes we wake up with new faces littering the yard. Rylee has even started to name them like they are her new friends.

If we let Karma outside, she pisses on them. Warning them this is her territory. And recently, Elijah has started to grow lion's mane and oyster mushrooms off their skin. I don't want to fucking know, so I don't ask. But I still wonder why he can't do this at his own fucking house, look at all this land.

"Do you smell that?" Elijah sniffs the air dramatically. Sid giggles in his arms. This should be good. I laugh as he continues, "Greta, did you shit yourself?" An unexpected roar of laughter bursts from my mouth.

I can feel anger radiating from her body. If she doesn't throw her walker at him at least once today, I'd be impressed. "Oh, you motherfucker. You know that's your pigs."

Rain comes to stand next to me. I wrap my arm around her shoulders and pull her close. Kissing the top of her head, my lips move on her hair. "You can tell me. I know you know."

The overwhelming excitement I have, to have another grandbaby, is really embarrassing, but I don't fucking care. She slaps my chest and looks up at me, mouthing, "Boy."

SID

Age Ten

"Sid. You need to sprinkle it around. Don't just dump it in." My dad huffs out a deep breath of annoyance. His eyes widen in frustration because he would rather just do it himself, but I want to learn. I need to!

"Sally, Millie, dinnertime," I shout as I begin to sprinkle the body parts around the perimeter of the pen. We've had pigs since before I was born but recently, Dad let me pick out two of my own to bring home and raise, and I take this responsibility very seriously.

"When did you name them?" My dad looks at me confused while twirling his bat in his hand mindlessly.

He is itching for violence. Mom said it's been a few days so he's a bit more 'testy' than usual. But I call it his kill twitch.

"Always. They are my babies like me and Blaise are yours and Mom's." Obviously. I don't get what he doesn't understand about the concept.

Then I ask, while scattering the last of the arm bits into the pen, "How did OG gran die?"

Dad looks at me, puzzled and sighs, "I killed her, Sid. I tell you this every time you ask." I do ask a lot, but I find it comforting.

"Sorry, I just like hearing the story, is all." I pout, pushing my lip out, and looking up at him.

He knows my games, but as Dad rolls his eyes, he gives in, my plan always works, "Fine, hurry up. I'll tell you when we go back inside." I'm jumping up and down, giddy with excitement, when I get an idea. A large grin adorns my face, as my eyes widen, replacing my previous 'poor Sid' pouty look. Glancing up at Dad, he seems uneasy about my swift mood change, concerned, he barks, "Go on then. What is it?"

Clearing my throat, I ask, "Daddy, can I kill too?"

The End.

Stay Tuned For...

Sweet SIN Slaughterhouse
The Devil's Society
A Sapphic Erotic Horror

SOME WORDS FROM KINS

If you want a sneak peak into the life of Darian and Cecilia, check out;

Phantasm by *Harleigh Beck*

Nathaniel and Delacroix's bromance is next level! Thank you to Ms. Harleigh Beck for letting our words and worlds crossover. I absolutely adore you!! Beck Kincaid Enterprises™ for life.

It was insanely important to me that the Domme Community was accurately represented in *Unholy*.

I bow down to the incredible, *Gwen Ellis*, my dear friend and member of the domme community, for helping me ensure this. For taking time out of your busy life to read Unholy, which is so near and dear to me, I say thank you! Thank you for allowing me the great honour and privilege of taking a glimpse into your world. I love you.

My Alpha/Beta Warriors - From when I start a book to finishing it, is maybe a 6 week span. Hello ADHD, have we met? I always wait until the last minute to start, but always finish on time, by then sleep is a distant memory, but it's fine. Thank you for always making time to read my roughest of drafts, providing feedback and cheering me on, whenever I have doubts. Words will never be able to express how grateful I am to have each one of you a part of my journey.

Sweet Rumi, my editor, my hero. I get so excited sending you the next installment of this series or whatever crazy idea I've had. Thank you for all that you do for me and my book babies. Thank you for taking a chance on me and my wild mind! Thank you... I just needed to say it once more - lol.

Daisie Mae, my proofreader. We have been friends for what seems like a lifetime. But really, when thinking about it long enough, it hasn't been as long as I thought. We have been through it together, the high highs to the low lows. Thank you for always taking care of my babies and cheering me on from the tallest rooftops!! You and Beks and lifers. You're welcome - haha.

And to my Street Team, the Bat Cave Bat Chat and all Little Bats and Queens!! I fucking love you. Thank you for everything you do. I am forever grateful. There is no me, without you! And Lucy, you are *that* bitch - haha. Inside joke!

Until the next one,

-Kins

ABOUT THE AUTHOR

Kinsley is a Canadian, Dark Romance Author who dabbles in Taboo, Forbidden, and is currently in her Erotic Horror Era. When she isn't plotting her next twisted book or watching true crime docs with her cats, you can find her working for the man. Reading. Or listening to Taylor Swift.

Make sure you follow Kins on her socials and sign up for her newsletter to see what is coming next!

authorkinsleykincaid.com

ALSO BY KINSLEY KINCAID

FORBIDDEN

Let's Play

Within the Shadows

Lessons from the Depraved

Haunted by the Devil; The Devil's Society

Sinner; The Devil's Society

Homecoming; The Devil's Society

Unholy; The Devil's Society

Sweet SIN Slaughterhouse; The Devil's Society - 2025

TABOO

Wrecked

Sutton Asylum

Dark Temptation: Part One

Ghost Dick; A Port Canyon Chronicle

Dark Temptation: Part Two

Lessons; An Extremely Fucking Taboo Extended Epilogue

Brothers Bond

Sick Obsession

Fuck Me, Daddy; A Port Canyon Chronicle - TBD

Taboo can be found via the authors' website.